Family Gumbo

Family Gumbo

By: LaShonda D. Johnson

Volume I

FAMILY GUMBO *volume one published by*

Bozznitti Presents
P.O. Box 1861
Temple, TX. 76503

ISBN: 978-0-615-33113-3

Library of Congress Control Number: 2010902189

First printing, March 2010
10 9 8 7 6 5 4 3 2 1
Printed in the United States of America

Unfamiliar

I have a huge family of cousins, nieces, nephews, uncles, aunties and in-laws too. Unfortunately, there is no bond, at least no further than my mom. I know this is wrong; I want close ties with my family and make new memories.

I wished for a family that did not hold on to wrong doings, grudges, and harsh feelings. I wanted the support to have been there and aid when one is going through it. But, it's far too much greed and jealousy and the feeling unsettles me because this is all within a blood line that's so broken, a non member can intervene between me and family and be treated with honor and loyalty.

I am weakened, by the thought and hurt by the feeling of being unfamiliar to my family. I want to share so much with, the very same members whom happen to share parts of my growth from young to old. Unfortunately, this can never be unless the envy is unleashed.

Fortunately if it's meant to be, God will prevail, until then I'm surrounded by individuals just holding various titles which fall under linking family together - and I submit to being unfamiliar and unknown within my family.

-LASHONDA JOHNSON

FAMILY (fam'.a.li.) n. parents and their children; the children of the same parents; descendants of one common ancestor; group of individuals within an order or subdivision of an order.

INGREDIENTS *(chapters)*

THE BEGINNING

The essence of time produced a spiritual connection between Justin and Shakira. This spiritual bond lead to a happy marriage in the year 2001, the month of September and yes, the day the nation came to a standstill, "the 11th!" Justin and Shakira did not know that at the time their supposedly unpredictable marriage was taking place in Las Vegas, a group of Terrorists was attacking the Twin Towers in New York. Justin, "The Philosopher he was known to be" was four years older than Shakira and had believed this was a sign of marital destruction. Justin well endowed with the knowledge of Theology, Anthropology, Business and Economics and the spirituality of "Jesus Christ himself!" Shakira in the blink of an eye realized this type of spiritual man it what she needed in her fragile structured life, although they were opposite in some ways. Justin was verbally aggressive but wisely used his vocabulary in a more diplomatic way, and had a confident voice of authority that implicated people to listen whereas Shakira more in line with "Border Line Personality Disorder"; was commonly known for being passive. One in the same was the hearts of the two who sought love and security, which they had understood to be a blessing from God. As the saying goes, "those two fallen Angels were a match made in heaven." Unfortunately, Justin and Shakira were unaware that they would be tested far more than what they expected.

Prior to Justin and Shakira's marriage the two had planned to have an informal wedding and then have a reception a couple weeks after. They figured that way all the families could come together and meet but Shakira's side of the family responded to the news of marriage rather negatively from the mother all the way down the family tree, expectedly telling her she should wait. Perhaps, they could not swallow the fact that Justin recently been released from prison after serving seven years on a non-violent conviction. Shakira's family never considered that Justin was sincerely looking to rebuild his life, with Shakira. Justin was a very honest person and was open and honest with Shakira from the beginning, and had asked Shakira to be open and honest with her family as well about his felonies saying, "They were to be his future in-laws and it was important they knew the truth". Nevertheless, it did not matter to her family that Justin chose to be honest about his past. All they saw was Justin hoarding in and living off Shakira, which did not matter to Shakira one way or another she just knew Justin needed her in his life and she needed him. Justin was not too pleased after finding out he been placed in the same category as the previous men that had crossed Shakira's path. Remarkably though, when Shakira's and Justin's paths crossed they knew their spiritual union was for a purpose bigger than they were, and did nothing to defer from Gods guiding light.

It was hurtful to Shakira and she was feeling as though she was in the middle torn apart like a piece of paper. She wanted her family, especially her mom to see what she saw in Justin. They saw nothing but an ex-convict. Which was puzzling because Shakira remembered when one of her uncles, his wife and three of his kids, which were in there late teens at the time, all of them were in jail at the same time, all held on different criminal charges that held drugs and assault. Even Shakira's father, who passed away from cancer when she was twelve, had served time in jail for murder. How soon did they forget about what was going on now, like Shakira's older cousin Marlene was involved in several relationships with men, including a hidden marriage that ended before her father or anyone new. Marlene's dirty laundry only came out because this derange man she had married refused to give Marlene personal belongings back to her, setting off a family response to this unresolved situation, which caused her family to promptly aid her. Shakira watch from the outside of it all; cops, bats, yelling and jail was the outcome. In another instance, Marlene was chasing down a sexually challenged man that had a woman on the side. In addition, to think that Shakira's character was the only one on trail in the family. Therefore, Shakira could not begin to understand why they would be so judgmental of Justin, when in fact her family had many skeletons in their own closets.

Shakira's family sure did not waste any time before Justin was the topic of her family's conversation, of course not in his presence. In Justin's presence, they would smile and talk but the mask behind the smiles told a different story. Her family, still, was refusing to treat Justin as part of the family, when he and Shakira showed up at family gatherings. Justin felt uncomfortable at times, but he went because he loved his wife. He knew she just wanted acceptance from her family. It was really odd, because the same members of Shakira's family that had something to say about her marrying Justin were the same members that hid their skeletons of being involved in illegitimate affairs or criminal activity of thievery, deceit, and lies. Nevertheless, no one gave the time of day to hold meaningful discussions with Justin about whom he was or who he had intended to become. After all, the only concern should have been if Justin could provide a future for Shakira and Hadea.

The ringleader of it all was Shakira's mom. If they wanted to know what was going on all they had to do was call Shakira's mom. She was the 411 person in the family, she can be reached at any hour and any day and give you the information needed.

All the kids in the family called her Nana BG and the adults treated her as if she were some type of Mob boss who is in charge and everyone jumps when she says jump. How was she ever nominated to be in this position was unknown. Assumed that Nana BG had all the answers and knew just what to say and do. A lot of the family relied on

Nana BG because she was safe. She was like a super citizen, never in trouble with the law, no drinking, and no drugs and she was always willing to help if she could.

To be fair, Shakira's mom was not the only gossiper in the family, she was the torch and the rest of the family carried it and added on what they thought was really going on.

None of the negative vibes that Shakira's family had about marrying Justin bothered her to the point of regrets. On the other hand, it did bother her because she loved Justin and her mom. Yet, her mom wanted her to live as she says. Besides, that did not call for a man at this time. Shakira was tired of loveless relationships and wanted to settle down. It was the blanket of bitterness that Shakira's mom wrapped herself in every since the death of Shakira's father, Shakira heard stories of her father being a cheat and liar up until the day he died.

On the other side, Justin's family had greeted Shakira with open arms. It was never a time when Shakira felt uncomfortable while hanging out with Justin's family. There was no judgments' against Shakira or her seven-year-old daughter named Hadea, they were family from the commencing.

Hadea and Justin hit it off from the very beginning, she loved him, and he loved her as if Hadea were his own. There was never a solid male figure in Hadea's life. Yeah....; her biological father Jeff had never played a huge role in her life, every since he married this police woman that would make all three of Charlie's Angels look bad; Jeff seemed to have no time for Hadea since he had his new family and all, so Hadea started seeing even less of her father. Unfortunately, there was no room in Jeff's life for Hadea but Shakira in 2004 had agreed to drop her full custody case and discontinued Jeff's child support payments for Hadea. Fortunately, Justin was now a very big part of Shakira and Hadea's life in order for Shakira and Justin to make such a decision.

Hadea had always been a happy child but since Justin came into her life and seized quality time with her, Hadea seem to have had an extra spark to her spirit. Unknowing to Hadea Nana BG had issues with Justin, which Hadea at this time did not see anything wrong with coming back and sharing with Nana BG the places she went and the things she saw, while enjoying herself with Justin and her mom. Nana BG would boil inside, because she disliked for someone else to make her first-born grandchild happy without her.

See, the problem with Nana BG is that she had been the added support in Hadea's life since she was born. Nana BG, Shakira and Hadea spent a lot of time around each other in the public's eye, where probably not a single person had recognized the attachment they shared but there was positively a strong attachment among the three. Sorry to say, what had once seemed unbreakable was soon to come to its dreadful end but certainly not without Nana BG putting up an emotional fight. Although Justin recognized Nana BG's attachment for Shakira and Hadea, he still was not looking at the picture in full focus at that point, because he naïvely continue to praise his marriage; saying, "he had finally found a woman that did not live up to her mother's expectations Thank the Lord."

As for Justin's side of the family, there were plenty of girls Hadea's age and they were now her cousins. Hadea been invited to do things with Justin's cousin Tami and her daughter name Beth, whom was a year younger than Hadea. She was an only child too. A few times Hadea stayed the entire weekend at her in-laws house and when Nana BG found out she had the nerve to question it as if Shakira was letting her daughter stay anywhere with some unknown strangers. Nana BG felt as if she was losing her grand child and her daughter. She did not look at the bond built between Justin and his family.

Hadea did not let her grandmother stand in her way; she was only a child trying to enjoy her new family. Sometimes it would be two or three days before Nana BG would talk to Shakira or Hadea. Her understanding of Shakira trying to stand on her on without her and build memories and traditions within her own home was often blurred. Still Nana BG had not taking time to sit down and get to know Justin, even though he was now her son-in-law. Although Nana BG had often talked to Justin, it was never a moment that she felt that she needed to know him as a person. Her outlook on a person was sight first then assumptions on whom they are. She mistook his humbleness for weakness, him being spiritual for being a religious fanatic as she called it.

Nana BG was very strong willed. She declared that she was always right about everything and everyone. She did not bite her tongue when telling someone about professing her glory on being right. Even though her horns would sometimes protrude, Nana BG would still help anyone if she could. She may complain a bit but she tried to make the lives of others less hectic but under one condition, you have to live under her rule of thumb.

Nana BG had no husband, her first marriage ended with her husband killed by his first wife. Nana BG told Shakira that his ex-wife shot him on a cold windy night after he was leaving a local bar, because she had just heard about him and Nana BG getting married. Her second marriage, which was to Shakira's dad ended when he was caught cheating. After that hurtful scene of infidelity, Nana BG had a bad taste in her mouth about men; saying, "All men are dogs and you can't trust them no farther than you can see them". Sadly, that is just what she had thought of Justin.

The first few months of Justin and Shakira's marriage were great. Their income had doubled, Shakira was just your average everyday call center supervisor and had been for the last four years; on the other hand, Justin had an entrepreneur spirit about himself, he had put together a plan to start a janitorial business. Eventually the business begin picking up more clients, which gave Shakira a opportunity to give her job a two week notice and focus solely on the business. Now owning and operating a business, Shakira and Justin had reasonably freed up some quality time. It was at these times Justin, Shakira, and Hadea would travel different places enjoying their family adventure every chance they got. Seemly, on rare occasions they would pop in to visit cousins, aunts and of course the moms of Justin and Shakira. However, our visits were not enough. There were some harsh feelings and words going around and it started with, "They thinking they are too good". At least this is what Nana BG put out there to her family. Justin's family could not say too much, because he had repudiated his family temporary while he was attending college every day. Shockingly enough, the same statement started floating off the tongues of a few members of Justin's family.

Little by little the envy, jealousy, and control among the families had started. In addition, evil was now knocking at the front door of Justin and Shakira's self-important souls.

JEALOUSY AND ENVY

Owning a business that is generating income, coming around to his tenth semester of college, working towards a Bachelors degree in Criminal Justice and Psychology, Justin was trying to do it all before his life's plans was altered after earning his AA degree. Determined to finish what he started, Justin not only for his self, but also for his wife and stepdaughter continued his education in investigations and CSI cases as well as learning theology and anthropology. His gift was natural; some would say his traits were of a Gnostic. Justin says, "as long as he remembers he has always been spiritual and followed God signs of life rather than mans. This was one of the reasons why Justin was misjudged, but mostly by family. His encounters with others lead them to see an intelligent, humble man who just wanted to be able to provide for his family.

As Justin carried a full load of classes and helping operate the business, Shakira was equally as busy with taking up slack in the areas that needed be. During this time, Hadea often spent the nights at Nana BG's house. Nana BG still had very much control and say so in what goes on in Hadea's life. Not once did she ever think to step down honorably from the responsibility and care that often tired her out. She was even being civil towards Justin but you can never tell with Nana BG, she was still holding back her sincere feelings. Justin questioned the actions of Shakira not stepping up to the plate more while dealing with her mom but she just brushed it off as it being okay. Justin would often talked to Shakira about how their lives would eventually be affected from the things to come if Shakira did not realize placing family values above spiritual values was totally against God's purpose.

Genuinely, Shakira had no reason to think that the negative opinion Nana BG had about Justin would eventually affect Hadea's feelings towards him. Shakira was still in denial that this was not a passing fade for her mom and her issues with Justin and continued to let Hadea spend a lot of time with Nana BG. However, in actuality, things were not as simple as she thought and they were more than she was willing to open her eyes too. The universe was starting to shine the light of grievance. Justin and Shakira were alike, they both longed for family closeness and structure. Justin's way of future stability had always included members of the family, unfortunately, if it was something they knew nothing about they thought of it as trying to be took, as if that what was expected for turning their backs on him.

Between both sides of the family, they knew the business was doing well and that Justin was completing his degree. They had incorporated jobs that would be able to pull in members of the family. Figuring that everyone can pull together and help build a system to work for all of them. Miraculously, Justin and Shakira's good intentions presumed useless. Their own families had started labeling them as Mr. and Mrs. no it all. They were looking for them to fall down the ladder. Their sincere help was taken has a pity handout. The expectations of having family support and added growth in their endeavors were missing.

Shakira's family, namely her mother thought that Shakira was doing too much and Justin not enough. She would often question Shakira as to how she felt about Justin going to school while she maintained the business. At the time, it was never a problem to Shakira. In fact, she never looked at it any other way than lending support to her husband for the benefit of laying a foundation. After all, it was not completely odd that a wife would work while her husband went to college or even a stay home father with a home business was not odd.

Justin's family was no better. It was not joyous that he was putting his life back together and being productive. When Justin's cousin Tami learned that he had returned to college the silent competition was on. She too hurriedly and enrolled in a few classes.

Her intentions were not pure and lying with her was the intimidation she had for Justin. This was her character. She saw what others were doing and immediately tried to do it faster and better. Justin could not even count on the happiness from his mom. Instead, she held on to hardened feelings about Justin returning to college. This was once her dream that she started. However, it was never finished the new beginning of her marriage and having a family directed her path in other directions. Not to mention three failed marriages.

In seeing how certain family members felt Justin and Shakira begin to back away. Month by month, year by year, Justin would tell Shakira family issue that would manifest. All their burdens begin taking a slight toll on everything they had worked for and the accomplishments they had earned. Never the less, thoughts about how Shakira's mom felt about her marriage begin to seep into Shakira's state of mind, causing a disturbance in her own home. Shakira was losing herself in the mist of her challenge for happiness; her insistence on wanting everyone to get along was a job in its self. The breeze of envy and jealousy was in the air. The more Justin had told her to remain with faith and live with God, the more Shakira pushed away. She was slipping into a hole of destruction.

The ties of Justin and Shakira were loosening. As always, Justin had been the voice of reason. The one who has long had the understanding of what it meant to live by what Jesus had professed. Not even Shakira remained planted and followed the footsteps of her husband. Bits and pieces of the gossip started reaching the ears of Justin and Shakira. Worst of all Hadea's attitude shifted toward Justin.

Her ears were hearing the negative outlook that Nana BG had towards him and following suite, she too made her mind up that Justin was the one taking her mom away. Not to mention, Nana BG had found the time to find and contact Hadea's natural dad. She had even taken Hadea to his house and letting him come to hers to see Hadea. It was never a problem to let Hadea see her dad; he needed to prioritize his dealings with his daughter. When Justin and Shakira both found out about this situation, Justin felt betrayed and Shakira was shocked to think that her mom would be so deceiving. When Shakira confronted her mom about the situation, Nana BG responded, "Hadea needs a relationship with her dad." Shakira's mom portrayed that she was only doing what was right for Hadea. Her claim also was that Hadea missed her dad a lot.

Shakira knew right off that her moms' intentions were far from doing what is right. Her intentions leaned more on the lines of trying to hurt Justin. Unquestionable, this was starting to take a toll on Justin. No longer could he keep Shakira on the right side of faith. Shakira was never a stand up type of person. She often let all her anger bottle up then explode like a shook up can of soda. The right things to say to stop from what was starting escaped her. Soon, she began to feel displaced in the marriage; she was a major part of the anger, envy, and jealousy brewing among her family toward Justin.

THE CAUSE

In the passing of five years' times were tough and there were road blocks that suddenly started to appear. Arguments between Justin and Shakira were frequent. They were mostly about what her mom may be capable of doing next. Shakira was thunderstruck, her thoughts seemed to be drowning in disbelief that this was her mom and her daughter causing mischief behind her back. Shakira's clarity distorted at the time made her feel as though she had to choose between her family and Justin. With Shakira, being mad at Justin, and going to her moms this only made her mom and Hadea happy but when Shakira returned home to Justin; Hadea and Nana BG would feel devoid of Shakira, because Shakira did not go to her moms' house to stay often. Hadea was old enough to see the distress in her mom, but she was not old enough to understand. Hadea's outlook was that if her mom got away from Justin then she would be okay. Hadea heard and was involved in adult business and she hung on to every negative word spoken of Justin from her mom and Nana BG so this is what made it right in her mind. Therefore she sought out full fledge to turn against Justin as if he stole something from her.

By this time, Shakira had turned into a ball of unsorted emotions toward everyone. Unfortunately, Justin had gotten the short end of the stick. Her unbalanced temper and the strange antics that always followed had Justin worried. Worried that his wife, his other half may have a disorder. She would jump out of the windows as if there was no front door. She would yell and scream at the top of her lungs and it did not matter what she said or who heard. After a few hours, she would calm herself, and then become apologetic for her uncontrollable out bursts. Justin would always stand there looking like a surprised manic after seeing his wife act as if she were an animal in the wild. Justin eyes would fill up with tears but like always, he was just too strong to let a tear drop. His words were no longer comforting to her. All he could do is pray and continue to strengthen her spiritually.

There was no one in Justin's family that he could lean on for advice. Confidentially, he did use his mom as a listening ear. Although Justin's mom did not dare say too much, for she knew her son was not going to allow anyone to bash his wife or his stepdaughter. After the conversation and the updates of what he was going through with his in-laws and his wife, Justin's mom would seem to morph into AT&T; reaching out to everyone. Therefore, this is how Justin's side of the family received their information and uses it as ammo against Justin.

Shakira could no longer hide behind what once was true happiness. She was going through the days as if she was outside of herself. Every day was a struggle to think and interact normally. It was lights on and no one home kind of thing with Shakira, the only difference she was still able to care for herself. She was often frightened because her thoughts were not her own and it was getting harder to control the eruption of the volcano inside her. Justin would find the time for the two of them to just sit and talk and he would always tell his wife; "Let me help you, just tell me what you are feeling". She could not; the only thing that would come out before the tears was a bunch of rambled thoughts and emotions with never a point as to what the real issue was.

Shakira's love for her mom interfered with her marriage from day one. She had let her mom in her marriage, instead of God. Shakira's love for Hadea was also an interference, as Hadea started being disrespectful to Justin, which Shakira never stopped it and neither did Nana BG. Shakira was beginning to believe every negative thing her mom was saying about Justin. Shakira had lost sight of the man in which she married. She knew him better than anyone did. Yet she never took a stand when she heard things about Justin that was not true. This was also the case when it came to her in-laws.

By now just about everything had hit the fan. Although neither of the two sides of the family ever built a line of communication amongst them, their intentions became all the same.

Shakira's label was Ms. Brainwashed. Which was confusing to Shakira, how could a wife, not battered or abused be called brainwashed for following her husband, the head of the household. Her mom felt pity for her, she felt as though her daughter could be doing better. Whatever *better* was to Nana BG? She expressed this throughout the family and they too drew their own explanations of dislike.

Not knowing all of Justin's family members, one-day Shakira's mom was overheard saying in the supermarket talking to another woman about how she could not stand her daughters husband and that she hoped that she leaves him soon. The person who heard that was an aunt of Justin's, so every word got around to Justin's family and then back to Justin. This was hurtful to Justin. He kept pleading with his wife to talk to her mom. That was not the battle; the battle was getting her mom to have an open mind. In which Nana BG did not have an open mind so it always lead to an argument, then a hang up of the phone. Rationally, Shakira opted for the easy way of just to ignore her mom and her antics.

Shakira's mom started keeping Hadea again; she claimed she was unsafe. It was unknowing at the time as to how she came by this claim.

Nana BG had spoken with Hadea's biological father and told him that he needs to step in. Shakira had lost several pounds due to stress; no one saw it as stress, they swore she was on drugs. Well, when one of Shakira's cousins saw her in the store they had the guts to ask her this absurd rumor.

As for Justin's mom, she was angry because she thought Justin had more money than he was letting on and was not giving her any. She expected lavish gifts of jewelry, trips, and money as he did in the past. That was when the cash came from gambling. Everything was legit now; Justin was not trying to waste time behind wrecked decisions that could hinder his life.

Justin's mom would periodically call the college admissions office to leave Justin messages to call as soon as possible. Justin's moms always looked for him to rush to her aid, although there was no emergency, either she would be gone before he got there, needed money or acted as if she stated that it was no emergency and that he just needed to contact her. Justin soon ignored her calls and messages. That just made her send different members of the family to the house to do a ride by and look, or call and act as if there was a bond of concern and well-being for him. Nana BG would call Shakira with a million and one question if all else failed. Once Justin was hip to the antics, he put his foot down and confronted each involved family member. All swear innocence and that he was *crazy*. This just gave them something to laugh for, they enjoyed seeing the demise of Justin, but as long as he was giving them something, Justin was the best in the world.

Through all the family dysfunction, Justin and Shakira still had each other and Justin deemed himself strong enough to not let it hinder him from completing school. He was nearly finished.

One day before picking up Justin, Shakira stopped by the post office to pick up the mail then headed to pick up Justin from school. As Justin came walking from between the Criminal Justice center and the Forensics lab and across the neatly manicured lawn of the college, Shakira slid over to the passenger's seat. The biggest bombshell of them all happened that day. It was not if they have not already had a lot on their plate to deal with.

Adjusting her seat belt and grabbing the mail. Shakira sorted through the mail, which most of it was for Justin or had something to do with the business. Until she got to a cream colored enveloped addressed to her from the States Child Custody Courts. Opening up the envelope and pulling out the letter to unfolded it and began to read.

Shakira had been official served with papers regarding turning over custody of Hadea to her natural father. This was an immediate dagger to her heart. Shakira was numb as she sat skimming over the white piece of paper, which held the words in bold black type: **Child Custody, Parental Negligence against a mino**r. Shakira had so many words to express but all she had the energy for was to let tears profusely roll down her face. Taking the paper out of Shakira's hand, while maneuvering the steering wheel of their SUV, Justin took a glance at the paper. Justin then replied; Damn Shakira, you tripping if you think Hadea's dad has a chance to take Hadea away. Come on Shakira I know you better than that and you know yourself so stop worrying about your family that's dispersing rumors about you.

Trying to talk instead of babble, Shakira looked at Justin and told him that she apologize for what he had been put through and if she had ever said or did anything that made him feel as though she did not love him, then she was so sorry.

Coming to a red light Justin reached over, and kissed Shakira, reassuring her that everything would be okay. Both engaging in a smile as the light turned green, the truck was once again, filled with only the music of the soft jazz channel.

As the SUV once again came to a stop and then to an accelerated roll, Shakira's breaking point had reached no return and to no thought, Shakira calmly unbuckled her seat belt and shifted in her seat, Justin gave no thought of Shakira's actions; they seemed none threatening. Then she was gone. The asphalt became an instead thread mill already in motion. Shakira tumbled several times with no control of her limbs. She came to a sliding stop as if she slid into home plate at a baseball game.

Justin screamed at the top of his lungs, No! Slowing down and looking through his rearview mirror, what caught his eyes would forever etch his mind.

In the middle of the street Shakira was lying on her belly. She could see the hazard lights on the SUV. She heard a voice-yelling Stop! Stop! She turned her head slowly to the left and started to scream. She seen cars coming down the street and the voice must have been trying to stop them back far enough. She yelled for Justin and then a hand was on her back. Justin was there, he was hysterical, and tears were streaming like an Amazon waterfall.

Focusing on having no feeling from her torso up, Shakira realized the way she was laying, which was in a sprawled out belly position. Shakira then noticed that she could not feel her left arm, which sent Shakira into a panic that must have blacked her out, because when Shakira awoke she was in the hospital.

Shakira had broken her left foot and left arm, along with lacerations and scrapes to her face. Shakira and Justin did not have many words between them. He just sat on her side and held her hand. He could not believe that in a split second he could have lost his wife. He did not know what to think or to say. How could he help his wife out of her deep state of depression?

THE EFFECT

Earlier from the hospital, Justin had called home to let Hadea know that they were running late and that they would be home. He could not find the words to tell Hadea that her mom would be arriving home as damaged goods, broken during shipment. He did tell her that mom was in a little incident and not to be scared or cry when she seen her. Justin gave the assurance to Hadea that her mom was okay.

Arriving home, Justin parked and opened the car door for Shakira so he could carry her inside. Upon entering Hadea pops out from her bedroom with a wide grin on her face. She was happy to see them. It was rare that she would beat them home. As fast as Hadea's grin appeared, it disappeared. Tears welted up in Hadea's big brown eyes; Shakira turned to Hadea and spoke in a low shaky voice, stop that crying Hadea, mom is okay. Hadea asked, "Mom what happened?" Shakira could not very well tell Hadea that she jumped out the car, but did tell her that she was hit by a passing car as she went across the street to the store, while waiting for Justin to get out of school. Which was likely, several times before both Hadea and Shakira had went to that same store and the intersection was busy, given that it was across from a college campus. Hadea sat for a long time right next to her mom and just held her hand.

The next couple of weeks of being temporary handicap became frustrating for Shakira and Justin but they eventually managed. The laceration above her eye had came along with a huge bruise that made Shakira look as though she had a pirates patch on. She had a cast on her arm and leg. This sounded as if she peg legged when she walked across the hardwood floor. Four days had passed since the "accident" and Shakira had not called to tell her mom. She was feeling a lot better and was going to call her that day.

Instead, Shakira got a call first. "I guess since I can't see you I can't see Hadea either," was the first thing to come out of Nana BGs' mouth. Hello to you too, was Shakira's reply as she rolled her eyes as she spoke. Shakira's mom started again as if Shakira said nothing at all. I just want to let you know that Hadea's dad wants her to stay the summer with him and I told him it was okay. Nana BG then said, "You just need to drop her off at my house and I'll take her there". Shakira responded, "For the entire summer, I don't think so". Shakira thought to herself, biting the inside of her lip, mainly to help seal her lips shut to keep her from saying the wrong thing. Shakira let a moment of silence past then asked her mom why would she set arrangements and then tell her later. There was never a response to that answer but Shakira did hear how she was wrong if she was not going to let Hadea see her dad and how Justin is controlling her. From that last word Shakira heard nothing but, "You are a fool!" and then a dial tone.

Shakira hung up the phone and just sat there in disbelief. Turning to Justin, Shakira just shook her head. Let me guess, your mom had something to do with the paperwork they served you. "I told you that she was doing all this because she does not like me." Justin said in an angered but hurt voice. Shakira could not understand why her mom could not see, that what she does to Justin, she is affecting her as well.

The decision was hard, but final. Hadea did not mind going to her dads', she knew at least she will get the attention she wanted, her dad will take her shopping, and she would be with her stepsiblings. To go to her dad was an easy way out for Hadea.

Anyway, this was better Hadea thought, she did not like Justin being around, at times to hear him speak seemed to have a burning effect on her, and she would go into a rage and break things, curse, and yell. Hadea has seen her mom go through stages of rage and hurt. Therefore, Hadea would mimic all she saw. Shakira would act as if she was in an award-winning movie, and Hadea seen this as her mother turning against Justin, which is all it took to give Hadea the green light to disrespect Justin even more.

Hadea was set to go to her dad's house. Shakira had asked Justin to take Hadea and drop her off. He told Hadea to make sure that her dad knew Hadea would be there in about thirty minutes. When it came time for Hadea to leave, Justin went in the bedroom where Shakira was laying down watching TV then said, "Shakira, I am about to leave to drop Hadea off do you want to ride?" Shakira had replied solemnly, no. Shakira felt as if she was losing her daughter to someone who been estranged from her throughout important periods of her life. The resentment and anger boiled inside her for Hadea's "donor" as Shakira often referred to him as. Shakira could not bear watching Hadea leave knowing that Hadea's joy was only an illegitimate visage to hurt her mom.

The next morning when Justin and Shakira woke up he had asked if she felt like getting out. Shakira felt as though she was ready to get out after her voluntary isolation had receded within a month. They stopped at Neutral Juice and got a smoothie. Shakira sat in the car while Justin went in and ordered. It was easier this way since she still had a cast on her leg and arm and was still trying to maneuver herself around on the crutches. They ended up at Shakira mom's house afterwards.

As Justin and Shakira pulled up, Shakira's mom had just opened up the huge picture window that she so often loved to sit in front of and yell out to the kids if they were getting too loud while playing. Shakira had just gotten out of the car when Justin handed her the crutches and her mom was now standing in the front doorway. Her eyes got the size of nickels and her skin looked clammy all of a sudden. "Hey!" Shakira spoke. "What happened to you"! Her mom exclaimed in a high pitch voice. Thinking on her toes, Shakira remembered the story she told Hadea so now she have to tell the same story to her mom. Even though Nana BG probably already knew from Hadea, she just wanted to hear it from Shakira, then to replay the words and actions later to see if the story is believable. Shakira's mom and Hadea were good at talking in codes and secrets about what goes on with Justin and Shakira. Secretly, Nana BG and Hadea made a pact between their self not to tell Shakira what they talked about, because she would only tell Justin. As Shakira made it up the steps and to the front door Justin was right behind her as he greeted his mother in law. Nana BG wasted no time, swiftly interrogating Shakira, as if Shakira had just committed a crime. Justin sat quietly and only put his two cents in every now and again. He did not want any parts of the lie told, but he did understand the embarrassment his wife was going through. Therefore, he left the ball in her court and just cosigned if she needed him to.

Nana BG grunted asking where Hadea is. Shakira looking to Justin as to say with her eyes, here is the game then slowly answered, "Justin dropped her off at her dads last night". Nana BG replied, "Oh so you let her go?" Shakira pleaded with her mom saying that she never said Hadea could not go over her dad's house. Shakira told her mom that she had no right making that decision for her. Shakira's mom instantly showed fury in her eyes and at that moment, Shakira backed off and hurriedly changed the topic to how bad her arm was itching. She asked for a hanger. Going for the change in topic Shakira's mom went and retrieved a hanger from the hall closet. She handed it to Shakira and Justin sat back and watched as she started with a story of how her friends' sons' daughter had a cast and she infected her arm. Stories and advice wanted or not was particular of Shakira's mom for as long as Shakira could remember and this was one of the reasons as to why they clashed so much. Her mom believed, "that if you have been advised of an experience than there is no need to go through it". Shakira seen things different, she preferred to experience things and learn from her own experience.

The visit was short but relaxing. Her mom was in her, I will smile and Tolerate Justin phase. Therefore, she was extra nice, fixing his plate and getting his drink. Shakira's mom really made it comfortable. Shakira was actually surprised and wondered how long this was going to last. Perhaps her mom remembered how filthy she had been on the phone towards Shakira and knew she had to leave all issues alone. Justin and Shakira said their goodbyes and then left.

Three weeks had past and even though Hadea called often and talked to both Justin and Shakira as if she really had, unconditional love for Justin the house was still lonely. Even their pet cat Nefey missed Hadea. In the early morning hours she would always scratch on Hadea's room door to be let in, unknowing that Hadea was not in there she would keep scratching until the door gets open, than she would hop on Hadea's bed and lay on her pillow cooing like a newborn comforted by its mothers scent.

The phone rings and Justin picks it up, it was Hadea, and she was crying. She told Justin that one of the older siblings had hit her with a belt and she is bleeding. Knowing that this would probably trigger his wife, he calmly told Hadea to call Nana BG to pick her up since she was closer to Hadea than they were. Shakira knew something and before she asked, Justin told her that the kids had a misunderstanding and Hadea wanted to come home so Nana BG was going to get her.

Later when Hadea called, Shakira picked up the phone. She learned Hadea was at her dad's house with her stepsiblings and his wife's sister, whom was the eldest, but still a minor. She told Hadea and her stepbrother to stop arguing but Hadea would argue her point when she feels she is correct. Hadea's words must have pushed a button, because a brutal whip with a studded belt left three small open cuts on Hadea's right leg.

Shakira was furious and the next day she called CPS and interviewed with them when they arrived at the house. CPS took pictures and took statements, CPS informed Shakira of a surprise visit to Hadea dad's house, and base on the finding of the case they would know how to precede further if needed. Now Hadea's dad not only had the case open in regards to Hadea but also another case for child neglect from the children in his home. Upon arrival of the surprise visit, neither his wife nor he was home and the sixteen year old was about four doors down at a neighbor's house. This left one infant, a three year old and a nine year old in the house alone. When Hadea's dad received a call from the Sheriff that was in his home at that very moment with CPS, Hadea's dad was enraged.

Hadea had wanted to stay with Nana BG after leaving her dads house and that is where she remained.

Nana BG was upset that her grandchild would be treated in such a manner and it was agreed that Nana BG was not to let Hadea go anywhere with her dad. It seemed like Hadea's dad not care too much anyway. Hadea told him she did not want to come back to his house and he did not make an effort to provide any other options for them to spend time together so their line of communication lessen from that day forward. Shakira had received in the mail a form to complete for the CPS case but for some strange reason the fulfillment of going through the process had vanished from her. It became more of a nuisance to deal further in this matter so she let it be.

Hadea was old enough to talk and let it be known that she did not want to go back to her dad's and at her comfortability Shakira gave her that right to voice herself, honoring what Hadea wanted. Shakira was thinking that by having her mom keep Hadea that this would alleviate a lot of confusing, but it was only the beginning of what was yet to come.

The time finally came for Shakira to lose her casts. Even though she held the memory of that day, that she nearly caused irreversible damage to herself, Shakira still had the scars across her face, but was happy that now her cast that held her broken bones was coming off.

No time too soon, Justin's graduation was this weekend. He did it. Of course, Justin did it with the acknowledgement of high honors, percentile specially. This was the news that needed to be conversed among the family quickly. Unfortunately, Justin had received no glory. It was not expected but it sure would have been nice, to have everyone come together and celebrate an achievement that wanted to be shared with each family. Shakira did not bother to tell anyone in her family, except her mom, only with the dry dream of her mom retreating some of her negative thoughts about Justin. Her moms' only response was, "Now he can get a job". Before Shakira could even think, her words rumbled out like thunder during a storm. Then it was her moms turn and this time they were face to face. Shakira never in a million years imaged that this blow out could be the end forever as far as a relationship with her mom. There were no punches of words withheld. It was probably a good thing too. Shakira heard it straight from Nana BG in the flesh.

Her mom admitted to telling Hadea's dad to put in paperwork so he can get custody of Hadea, she admitted to telling family members that she suspected Justin and Shakira was on drugs. During that time, CPS did go out to check Shakira's home out and talk with Hadea and Justin. Now she finds out that her mom was behind that. Shakira was hurt, most of all that Nana BG had allowed Hadea's no good dad to come back around the family and destroy the emotional bond built between Hadea and Justin. Never before has Shakira been taken to the brink of disgust for her mom. She never cursed in front of or to her mom until now, and now she could not take any of it back. With Hadea crying because of all the yelling between Nana BG and Shakira, and Shakira crying out of anger and hurt, Shakira stormed out of her mom's house with Hadea in haul. Yelling out behind Shakira her mom stated, That Shakira was stupid and she knows that Justin pushed her out the car; she was not in any accident. Shakira kept walking as if she heard nothing, it was pointless to say anything further, her mom's words, and actions were the true entity of evil at that time. It was best to high tail it away from there as fast as possible.

Once Shakira made it home she told Justin everything, he did not want to say I told you your mom did not like me. However, Justin knew a little light would shine on the dark, leading Shakira to acknowledge that her mom was behind a lot of gossip and hatred that she diligently worked on to smut Justin even if it did mean hurting her own daughter.

Graduation day was here. Despite what just has happened Justin and all the evil intentions created by his mother in law, did not dampen this day for Justin at all.

It was a total surprise when Shakira and Hadea had waken before him and had a cake of congratulations, they must have been up for quite some time, there was about thirty multi-colored balloons that covered the living room floor. Justin was dumbfounded, he had no idea, and he did not even know when Shakira had found the time to get this together during this time of her entangled mind. Hadea had a surprise of her on for Justin, she made him a card, and a key chain made up of his favorite colors that had a gold letter "J" placed right in the center of her creation.

Upon arriving at the graduation ceremony Justin had to immediately get dressed and go through one last rehearsal. Shakira and Hadea found two chairs in the third row and sat down. Looking around, Hadea spotted Justin's mom. She was with one of Justin's aunts. They all made eye contact and Shakira waved hello, her mother in law beckoned for Shakira and Hadea to come over to where they were sitting. Not really wanting to move she did anyway. They made it over to their new placement of seats and waited for the ceremony to start. The ceremony started with the special honorees. When they called Justin's name, Shakira tried to have the loudest cheer out of the other eight hundred and fifty cheers that filled the room. Nevertheless, Hadea beat her by far; she has always had a heavy but projective voice. Justin's aunt leaned over to Shakira and said, "My nephew is handsome. I am proud. He did it! He did it!" Yes he did I am proud of him, Shakira replied as her eyes filled and glistened as dew drops on flower petals. She was happy for Justin. She was the only one who knew he was serious. Serious about life, God, family and being able to say that he has found life. Yeah, Shakira was about the only person who knew how much this accomplishment meant to Justin.

The ceremony lasted for about an hour and a half. Justin and Shakira had already agreed as to where they would meet since the crowd was going to be tough to get through. Shakira told her mother in law and Justin's aunt where to meet Justin. Shakira took Hadea's hand and mingled their way through the crowd of cheering bodies to meet Justin. He was there already waiting. Hadea ran and gave Justin a hug. She was smiling almost as hard as he was. Shakira caressed Justin's shoulder and on her tiptoes, she gave him a kiss. I love you she whispered as she looked into his eyes. Justin replied, "I Love you to Babe".

Justin's mom and aunt finally made it. His aunt was the first and only one of the two to congratulate Justin and give him a hug. Justin's mom said the ceremony was nice and she liked the speeches. To Shakira's surprise Justin's mom asked what they were going to do next but Shakira never heard his mother say, "I'm proud of you or something." Justin knew his mom had bitterness inside of her. Even knowing this Justin loved his mom, it was nothing in the world he would not do for her. Besides, this is nothing new, just something more added to the way his mom acted toward him. Most mothers would help build, she looked to destroy. Over the years and still now this was something Justin never understood and he never got an answer. Justin knew he did not have the heart to mistreated any of Shakira's family members, yet there was so much intimidation, greed, jealousy and competiveness that they showed towards him. Nevertheless, he did not let this hinder him. With or without family by his side Justin was determined to make a huge difference in his life.

THE MANIPULATION

A few months after graduation, the Criminal Division at the District Attorney's Office offered Justin a position within; uncomplainingly, Justin accepted. Because the District Attorney's Office did a very extensive background check and conducted a physical training test, it would be at least two to three months before Justin started. Justin was comfortable with his decision. He knew that there was another plan in motion.

Justin and Shakira's business started running a little rocky. The two major accounts they had, the same person had owned them. It turns out that she had been embezzling money from her company, forcing bankruptcy on one and the bank taking the other. Therefore, those accounts were lost. They still were bringing in enough to cover the expenses and if need be they did have some money in savings to fall back on.

Hadea was now officially a teenager and Shakira at times wanted to strangle her. Hadea was becoming even more disrespectful and not just towards Justin, but toward Shakira too. Nana BG was in Alabama. She only had the one brother and his family living in the same city as her. The majority of Nana BG's family lived in Alabama including her other brother and her mom. Therefore, she went every year.

With Nana BG gone, Hadea had nowhere else to go and get away from her mom and Justin. One thing did remain the same about Hadea; she kept her school grades and GPA up, and stayed active in her school activities. Besides all the drama Justin, Shakira, and Hadea still shared some good times. Then there were other times, Justin spent pulling Shakira and Hadea apart from a knock down drag out fight. At times, Justin thought he was a bouncer at a bar.

Shakira really had not spoken to her mom that much since she left. She called her a couple times since she got to Alabama. It was about 9 a.m. Shakira's time and noon in Alabama when her mom called. Already knowing it was her mom from the caller id Shakira answered the phone, "Hey mom". "Well good morning." She replied. Shakira and her mom talked for thirty minutes before they had any disagreements. Nana BG played her hand of drama first, she said, "That Hadea called her a couple of days ago and said Justin had grabbed her arms and would not let her go and you didn't do anything". Shakira stated boldly, "That's right, I didn't". Justin asked Hadea to wash dishes and she ignored him. Hadea went into character from then on. She talked and acted as if Justin and Shakira owed her something. Deliberately, when Hadea ran her revision of the events to Nana BG she left out that part.

Shakira begin to explain to her mom the full details of the incident. Starting with how she was telling Hadea about her attitude and its need for correction. Of course, this angered Hadea and gave her the power to say fine, she will wash dishes and the nerve to start breaking the dishes that were in the sink. Shakira had her mom on the speakerphone; Justin kindly interrupted and explained the second half of that morning's dysfunction. Speaking in a passive manner, Justin picked up the story of him entering the kitchen and asking of Hadea to clean up her mess. Never raising a voice or a hand to Hadea, Hadea started yelling. Justin was not her dad, then to salt the wound even more, Justin told his mother in law how it crushed him to hear Hadea say that nobody in this family will ever approve if him. Justin went on to let his mother in law know that after those words he was walking away from Hadea when she charged him, swinging her arms as if they were propellers. That is when he grabbed Hadea and told her to calm down. Hadea then started calling Justin all kinds of names and cussing. Jumping in the conversation Shakira said to her mom, "Mom you taking it as if I'm letting Hadea get abused". Shakira's mom always had a bit of an anger problem and immediately she started belittling Justin as a man to Shakira, "his wife and her daughter".

Nana BG stated that Hadea told her that they were on drugs and spend all the food money on getting drugs, which is why they rarely had any food. Nana BG also said that Hadea told her that Justin was beating Shakira. Shakira again shocked by the words that were coming out her moms' mouth. Everything Shakira's mom was hiding was coming out and Shakira wanted to hear it all. After this, her final decision would be to disassociate herself from her mom. As Shakira and her mom went back in forth, in octaves that would shatter any piece of precious crystal, Shakira learned that Hadea not only had secret conversations with Nana BG but with her dad and anyone else who listened.

For quiet sometime, Hadea had been going around bashing her stepfather and her mom. She was telling lies against Justin, in hopes that this would break up the marriage between him and her mom. Hadea had all the adults fooled. Instead of confronting Justin and Shakira about the far fetch stories told, Nana BG and other adults planned their own sneak attempts to help Hadea get away. The torment ended in Shakira's mom saying that she will do anything in her power to get custody of Hadea and then the dial tone of the phone connection ending was the only thing left, causing vibration to Shakira's eardrum.

Shakira was disappointed in Hadea, and she felt no reason to call Hadea out of her room and expose her cruelty, she would just lie anyway. Hadea stayed in her room for most of the day. This explained many of the stares Justin and Shakira endured as they went to Hadea's school functions, the being out casts at family functions.

Justin and Shakira lingered around the house, Justin was sitting at his desk doing some online research, and Shakira was watching TV close by. Hadea had entered the room in which they both sat. She stood there for a moment in silence as if to reading how the atmosphere was in there. Hadea started her words carefully as if not to say the wrong thing, she knew she was in hot water from Nana BG's earlier. She said that she had wanted to stay with her dad. Her claim was that if she left then maybe things would be better. Both Shakira and Justin tried to explain to her the circumstances involved in her actions. It was an understatement from Hadea when she said she understood, because she really did not. Shakira questioned Hadea's loyalty and morality toward what she had done to Justin, to her. All she could say was that she misses her dad and wants to stay with him. This time Shakira had no tears or remorseful feelings to Hadea wanting to stay with her dad so she obliged and asked her when she wanted to leave.

Logically, if timing was not anything, it was now as Justin and Shakira heard a knock at the door. Justin got up; he looked through the peek hole of the door. He motioned for Shakira to come to where he was. He then, opened the door. It was two officers and Hadea's dad was behind them. May I help you? Shakira asked. The officer spoke as he turned the volume down on his radio, are you Shakira Barnes? Yes. Well we received a call stating possible child neglect here. What, Shakira almost jumped right out of her skin. She visualized her hands around the neck of Hadea's dad. The nerve he has to come to my house with this mess. All it was was a ploy for payback for Shakira sending CPS to his house. Shakira said nothing further and called Hadea to the front door. She had refused to come. Therefore, they let the officers in. Shakira expressed to the officers that Hadea's dad was not welcomed into their home, so the officer ask Hadea's dad to remain outside on the porch. Shakira lead them to Hadea's room. They asked

Hadea if she was okay and does she feel safe. Now was the time Hadea needed to speak up and say something. All she did was shrug her shoulders and answer in a pouty tone yes or no and I don't know.

Turning to come out the room Shakira and the officers entered the living room hallway. They asked to speak with Shakira outside. She was glad that Justin was right along with her, exiting the door. One of the officers, which were a female, turned and said to Shakira that Hadea's dad had a complaint that Shakira did not follow the shared custody order. Shakira was ready and more than willing to confront this issue. First off, as she started in a confrontational manner, the custody order in which you are talking about has been in place since Hadea was five years old and never once has her dad pushed the issue of seeing her unless she called him or it was her birthday. She has always had the right to see him. Shakira went on to explain the scenario of CPS called in against him. Shakira told the officer that if Hadea wanted to go with her dad right now she could. By this time, Hadea was standing in the doorway and Shakira asked her if she wanted to go with her dad since she did say she wanted to live with him. Hadea said no, turned, and went back to her room. Well, there you have it she does not want to go, however Shakira stated, earlier that day her and Justin had a conversation about Hadea going with her dad and if that was not what Hadea wanted to do neither her or Justin would force her to go with her dad.

Turning to Hadea's dad, the officers explained that they could not make Hadea go if she felt like she was being neglected or in any danger. They advised him to go back to family court and get the order revised. Each of them went to their cars and the curtain peeking neighbors slowly backed away from their windows.

Justin was silent through most of that encounter that just took place. Not because he was lost for words, but because he and Shakira had already spoken of this moment playing out the way it had just done. Justin knew the personalities of Hadea and Nana BG better than Shakira. Each time he had predicted the next stunts played by them and so far, he was on a role on being correct. Yet in all this was all surreal to Shakira, never in her wildest dreams did she think that her mom and daughter would be so diligent in working for evil and acting as if they were victims.

After the emotional storm was over Shakira open Hadea's room door went right in and asked her, "Hadea you had the opportunity to go with your dad why didn't you take it?" Hadea shrugged her shoulders and said nothing. Shakira was hurt and fed up; she told Hadea that it would be best if she arranged with her dad to go live with him until Nana BG returned from Alabama.

The next morning they had another early morning surprise. It was Nana BG, she had gotten on the first flight home and was now on Shakira's door step beating on the iron screen door as if she was being chased. Shakira opened the door only to be face with her mom's loud and hostile tone followed by her razor sharp tongue, "I told Hadea's dad to call the police and come get her what is she still doing here!" Shakira stepped in the way of her mom heading to Hadea's room saying, "the police and her dad should have told you that they have no grounds to take her, besides if she really wanted to go she had the chance to do so yesterday." Hadea came out of her room, ran, and gave Nana BG a hug. Nana BG told her to go pack her clothes and whatever she needed, she was going to take her to her dads' house. Hadea quickly turned and was acting anxious. While Hadea was getting her stuff together Nana BG had a few more choice words to say about Shakira and when Justin came out of the bathroom, stepping into all the commotion she laid into him as well. Justin's self-control was far more disciplined than Shakira's was; he just sat and listened to all the screaming and name-calling. Each time Justin waited until he thought she was done, he started to respond but that fueled Nana BG even more. It was if the sound of Justin's voice that sent her over the edge.

By this time, Hadea had come out her room with two overnight bags and her backpack. Do you have everything you need? Nana BG asked. Hadea responded, "Yah Nana". "Let's go!" Nana BG said, as she directed Hadea to say bye to "her silly momma and Shakira's dirt bag husband". Hadea knew she was not really supposed to repeat Nana BG's words, so she just waved bye. Again, Shakira and Justin left with nothing but sharpened daggers in their backs as they watched Hadea and Nana BG go out the door.

Shakira had not heard from Hadea in about seven days. When Hadea finally called she acted as if she was having the best time of her life. Hadea talked about how she has all her stepsiblings over there at her dads. Shakira knew that this was a charade, although Hadea was happy to be in a home with other kids, being she was the only kid at home with Shakira and Justin. Getting to know her dad's family was exciting to Hadea at first, until Hadea noticed she was not receiving enough attention from her dad as she did in the beginning.

Before Shakira and Hadea finished their phone conversation, Hadea did mention that her dad wanted her to go to the school of his choice instead of attending the school of her choice; which was the same school she had attended the year before. Even though Shakira thought that it was odd to take Hadea out of her old school, she told Hadea that she needs to discuss this with her dad, and if she is going to be living under his roof, she needs to abide by his rules. Hadea sullenly answered okay. Shakira told her daughter to pep up; this was her chance for Hadea and her dad to get to know one another. A change was sometimes challenging to Hadea and she could become verbally unpleasant and if her dad had knew her, he would had known that he was brewing up a verbal altercation between him and Hadea. This was something he would eventually find out for his self.

The weeks went by and the altercations had started. Hadea begin calling once a week to her mom, which turned into daily calls. No longer, did she want to be a part of her family that knew nothing about her nor did she know anything about them. She was frustrated with not having her own room and having to rumble through packed clothes because there was no room for her clothes in a dresser or a closet. She was tired of being stuck in the house with the younger kids; a lot of the care for them fell on her, while the other two eldest came and went when they pleased. It was hard for Shakira not to say, "I told you" but she refrained from doing so each time she heard Hadea's complaints.

It was around 10:30p.m. When Hadea had called her mom, she was crying out of anger, she was yelling. Once again, her disappointment had settled in about her dad. Shakira was trying to calm Hadea down and find out what happened this time. Hadea told her mom that her dad made a statement saying, Hadea old life with Shakira, Nana BG, and Justin was over and he would do anything to keep her away even change the school she attended. Hadea's dad was adamant about changing her school. He did not care that she was at a 3.9 GPA, that she was involved in choir, band, and a counselor for a teen mentor group. It did not matter to Hadea's dad, because Hadea's life was being built without him and now he seen an opportunity to become a part of her life.

When Hadea expressed her dislike, towards the decision she was upset and cursing, you could tell her heart was torn; suddenly Hadea acted as if she was a Hurricane and went through the home destroying everything in her pathway. When Hadea got like this

Shakira knew Hadea's dad did not know how to discipline her.

Although Hadea was a bit of a drama queen at times, Shakira knew that this was real. Hadea was upset and she felt for her but during the phone conversation Shakira told Hadea that she needed to go grow up, this was her decision to live with her dad, and she just needs to talk to him instead of getting upset. Hadea pleaded to her mom to come get her. Shakira wanted to bail her only baby out, but she would not let herself do so. She had to give Hadea tough love. Hadea finally gave up asking and said that she is running away and if her dad tried to stop her, she was going to stab him. Shakira ignored Hadea's comment and told her to go lie down and they will talk in the morning. Hadea asked, "Then will you come get me?" Shakira remorsefully responded, "We'll see babe." I love you, Shakira told Hadea. Love you to mommy.

Hadea's dad had never experienced this side of his little girl and perhaps he would have known it if he did not try to make up for the absences in her life through material belongings and trying to be Hadea's friend instead of her dad.

Jeff, Hadea's dad, did not know of her rage she has inside, which is provoked when someone makes her angry. Hadea's words can be as vicious as a dog attack. Shakira felt bad for Hadea; however, as sick as it was, she was happy that Hadea was taking her dad through it. Hadea played on the fact that she can get whatever she wanted, so she asked for what she wanted, and she got it. Hadea was the one Jeff felt so guilty about for not being in her life, for the simple fact that out of all his kids, Hadea was his twin; the only difference she was female. Hadea's actions were hurtful and her words cut in deeper into him that night. Hadea told him that he was never a father to her and she considers Justin to be her dad. He never imagined that Hadea would say things to hurt him intentionally.

By morning, you best believe Shakira's phone was ringing early, Justin answered and it was Hadea. She sounded like she was in good spirits. Justin asked was she okay? Hadea answered, "Yeah, I'm with Nana BG, she came last night and got me so I'm going to stay with her." Justin just handed Shakira the phone and said, "Shakira ask Hadea where she is." Shakira grasped the phone, Hadea you all right. Yeah Nana BG came and got me last night, Hadea replied.

Shakira was livid; again, her mom intervened and went against her words. This was one of the main reasons as to why Hadea is so disrespectful towards her and Justin. Shakira told Hadea to give the phone to Nana BG, as soon as her mom got on the phone Shakira in unsusceptible words let loose on Nana BG; she still remembered that this was her mom so she was holding back. The rumbling of her moms' voice interrupted Shakira as she spoke in a rough tone, "Some people don't need kids and you one of them!" "You have forsaken your daughter for some no good man!" "He doesn't love you and he isn't going to amount to nothing, you are stupid!" "I got Hadea and you don't worry about it!" "You lucky I didn't call CPS on you like I did before!" Shakira was hurt; she slammed the phone down as the tears ran from her eyes. Justin pulled Shakira to him and held her tight. It took a few hours after this mighty blow before Shakira snapped out of her commonly depressed mood.

One good thing from the abrupt decision made by Nana BG is that Shakira's mind was at ease knowing Hadea was with her mom, Shakira knew her mom was not going to go for a lot of Hadea's mess.

The punches did not stop there for Justin and Shakira. The business was no longer producing enough for expenses. They would need to get a job. Bills were stacking up and everybody wanted their money.

They would have been okay if Justin's mom were not so hateful and jealous trying to prevent her son from making something out his life. Justin had received a letter in the mail stating that he would not be getting the position with the District Attorneys' Office due to the interview and information given on him by an interviewee. Normally they do not disclose the person, who squealed like a pig. Carelessly, who ever typed the denial letter added the name accidentally, and then they used a black pen to line through the name. God must have wanted Justin to see who this person was. Justin came up with an idea to make an imprint of the typed letter by making it appear on the blank sheet of paper underneath it. It was faint but clearly legible enough to see the letters form, Jeanette Davis. That was Justin's mom. He was shocked. He now had proof that his mom was trying to ambush his goals. There was no telling how much other damage she had done. After all, she did know many influential people within the judicial system.

Justin was so angry that he found himself already listening to the rings in the phone, he did not remember dialing and wondered now if this was the right number. His answer was confirmed when his mom answered the phone in her melodies voice. Justin played it cool and started out with plain old casual talk. He asked how she was and what has she been up to. His mom talked as if she had no care in the world. Justin told his mom how the position he was confident about denied him. She acted surprised and asked why. Justin explained that one of the interviewee's gave some negative feedback against him. Without hesitation Justin's mom asked, "Who was it, do you know the people they interviewed? Justin wanted to scare her straight of her evil. He knew that if he exposed his mom publically of her wrong doings she would be embarrassed. That would be the ultimate for her, so instead he told her that there is a process to find out who the person was that replied with a negative statement against Justin. He also told her that he has spoken to an attorney who advised him of having a good deformation of character case with enough proof to win. Justin told that he was already pursuing this matter and will go public with it. The more Justin told his mom about this matter, his story become believable to Ms. Davis. In an attempt to defer Justin from pursuing the case, Justin noticed immediately, his mom shooting out statements of doubt from her mouth; claiming Justin could not get that type of classified information and someone was misleading him.

Justin felt freed of a burden, he now knew the truth about his mom, and as natural as it came for Justin he then began a conversation with his mom speaking in a spiritual sense and not in physical sense. She endured it for about sixty seconds than like a dark entity, she exploded and said, "I don't want to hear no God stuff and you could not tell me anything because you are just a criminal with dreams!" Ms. Davis then hung the phone up.

His moms' response was no shock to Justin, there were other times before when his mom acted out, so Justin knew his next move and that was to treat her as he had in the past; distance his self from her. Justin felt like it was in his best interest to start at that very moment.

THE BOTTOM

Justin felt as if he let his wife down. Although Shakira did not say much about Hadea being gone, Justin knew she was hurt. It showed in her face, life was riding her like a Jockey riding a horse in the Kentucky Derby. Justin's hands tied behind his back; felt it was nothing he could do. Even if Hadea were, there it would be a strain and added pressure. She would have needed pocket money, clothes, school activity money and the list could go on, especially with being a teenager. Shakira and Justin were out of work so they did not have the extra money at the time. Nana BG covered the majority of those expenses until Shakira was able find employment.

Justin and Shakira both had been applying for several types of jobs for the last few months and neither had a lead on a position, which something was strange about that. They had applied with companies whom listed that they were hiring. The positions that each of them applied for, they met the qualifications and had enough work experience, but that seem to have no significance. All that came from the hundred and twenty day job search was two interviews for Shakira and one phone interview for Justin, still no position for either of the two.

Justin and Shakira did have two thousand dollars saved up for a rainy day but had now spent half of that leaving them with about nine hundred and ninety five dollars. A financial slump had occurred in their lives and Justin had to know if Shakira was going to ride it out. Justin never doubted that Shakira would not stay, but since this was a major change and with everything else going on, he figured that, he had to be fair and give her an option.

Justin saw that it was no use sinking money into paying the bills and piecing together rent. It was not enough to pay anything in full. They were already facing eviction and the lights should have been off; but by the graces of God, they were still on. Justin sat and talked to Shakira; they had to start planning on what to do. Justin had an idea; he asked Shakira how she felt about moving to a different state. It was no problem for him; he had lived in several different cities with no family around. However, he knew Shakira had always been in the same place as her mom. Then there would be Hadea, Shakira was not about to leave her no matter what. Shakira was excited about the whole idea. All she needed to know was when and where. The plan was to take care of all that was there first. They had decided to move to Washington. Justin had some connections working in one of the Forensics departments. He also belonged to a brothering association; its main chapter was located in Washington, and Justin had spoken with the president and some of the associates of this chapter. This looked as if this would be a good chance for Justin and Shakira to start over and begin a new life without the drama. With Shakira's skills, she would not have a problem finding a job. Shakira was ready to take control of her life, as well as Hadea's life; without Nana BG having a hand in saying so.

Justin and Shakira had to plan and prepare fast. They rented a storage unit and stored items in there that they wanted to send for later. They got a P.O. Box. They looked online for housing and found a duplex that was affordable, they had spoken with the property owner already in Washington and told her about their transition, and she agreed to hold the place for them with a deposit sent via money gram to her in two weeks. That was great because it gave them time to get some extra money before spending money.

September 11th was here, this should have been the day Justin, and Shakira was celebrating their seventh year anniversary. Nevertheless, it was a court day for the eviction. The day for Justin and Shakira was an early one.

They were well prepared. It was not a matter of eviction but what did matter was that this eviction did not go on their credit report. They felt they owed nothing base on the fact the property owner did not comply with several housing codes and Justin and Shakira were able to prove this with the documented evidence of problems that occurred throughout their stay in the duplex. As it would have it, the graces of God were on their side. They did not have to pay the property owner anything and the eviction would not be place on their credit report; the judge also granted them the stay in their place for 60 days.

Relieved the Municipal process was over, Justin and Shakira went home to enjoy their special day. They exchanged cards and splurged on takeout food. One of the reasons Justin and Shakira fit so well together. Neither of them expected expensive gifts. Both of them were simple and humble people, just being together, made them happy.

Hadea called and asked if she can have Nana BG bring her over to drop something off. Shakira had not seen Hadea in a few weeks and had talked to Hadea on three different occasions, so this was a nice surprise to have her come by. Just like clockwork, Nana BG and Hadea pulled up in exactly one hour in front of the house as promised. Hadea jumped out as soon as the car came to a stop. Nana BG never looked once at the houses front door as if she had side blinders on only see what was in her front view. Shakira did not expect her mom to get out the car, but she did want to acknowledge her moms presence. Hadea came into the house, gave her mom a hug and with the same enthusiasm Hadea gave Justin a hug too. She wished them both a happy anniversary as she held out a black and gold gift bag. Inside was a candle in the form of a man and a woman. The male figure was kneeling as he embraced the female figure by her waist. Hadea had even bought a card for them. Hadea was a thoughtful child, her heart tried to be in the right place most of the time; but Nana BG had this control over Hadea that would reprogram her to act differently towards a person upon Nana BG's command. Hadea spent about thirty minutes visiting with Justin and Shakira, before Shakira remembered that Hadea left Nana BG sitting in the car. Even though Hadea said, it was okay, Nana BG told her to take the time she needed. Out of consideration, Shakira told Hadea that she had better go. However, they can plan something for the weekend and they can spend more time together then.

There was still no contact between Justin and his mom. He did hear through the family grapevine that she was doing well. She had her bag of tricks still open; she was bashing Justin throughout the family. Truth or not she was telling it all. There was not much truth told by his mom, so she improvised and adlibbed quiet well. The big story going around was that Justin was too smart for his own good. Justin had imagined the laughter that came with the story of not getting the position at the District Attorney's office. The way Justin found this out was through his cousin Jermaine. Jermaine's mom and Justin's mom were sisters; Jermaine's relationship with his mom was close. Therefore, when Jermaine's mom and aunt got together and talked, his aunt would tell her son everything said about Justin. Justin did not fully trust Jermaine either, he was one to play both sides and everyone knows that if a dog brings a bone he will carry it too. Meaning Jermaine was joining in on the conversation about Justin even though he knew it not to be true, then he would turn around and tell Justin the stories that were going around the family about him, as if to be doing Justin a favor.

The transition was going as planned, until one day when Hadea was visiting. Shakira had let it out the bag that they were planning a move. Her reasons for telling Hadea, was to get her prepared mentally for this move. This was to be a new beginning for them all and Shakira was hoping that Hadea felt the same. The news of hearing about the move was not what Hadea wanted to hear, but she heard the happiness in her moms' voice and adjusted to what she thought her mom wanted to hear. This only opened an assortment of problems. Once back in the care of Nana BG Hadea could not wait to tell the news of the move. When she told, you best believe that Shakira's phone was ringing by that evening. To no amazement, Hadea's dad told Shakira that she could not take Hadea out of the state, because the courts would not allow it. Shakira's mom knew that Shakira was not suppose to take Hadea out of the state because of a standing custody court order that Hadea's dad implemented against her when he tried the first time to gain full custody. Shakira's mom was being selfish. She did not want to lose her grandchild as she put it. On the other hand, Shakira's mom knew they had to move in a matter of days but she did not care, not seeing her grandchild when she wanted was an absolute must to stop from happening.

This time Shakira was not going in for the battle with her mom, but she was staying firm. Shakira tried to be as mellow and mild mannered with the delivery of her words; maybe her mom would keep it peaceful. Once again, Nana BG subjected Shakira to her verbal abuse.

Shakira had no say so in the raising of her own daughter. Shakira took it now; as if her mom thought she was slow mentally and *needed* her help to care her Hadea. It was now that she knew she was unable to stop what she created. It was a diseased bond by allowing her mom to intervene one too many times with the decisions about Hadea. What was she to do now to turn it around?

The domino effects of falling down the ladder begin to play out. Money was not coming together as planned and with not enough money, there was not going to be a move. There was no family to offer a helping hand. Justin and Shakira waited out there days in their near empty house. They had sold some of their household items having yard sales. Justin and Shakira earned a good profit from their material possessions, in a time of needed cash.

The bulk of it came from selling the SUV, they were desperate and needed to part with it; gas was too high and the registration was coming up in a month.

Hadea was no longer calling like she was, but Justin had seen Hadea and Nana BG riding pass the house a couple of times, both times they were caught off guard, it was not expected for anyone to be outside. Hadea hands waving vigorously, as if she was on top of a parade's balloon float. Justin would wave back to Hadea as he watched his mother-in- law drive by looking straight ahead.

There was no contact from Justin's mom. Jermaine was calling and awful lot though. Justin suspected that he was only gathering information so he could go telegraph to his mom and then from his mom to Justin's mom. So Justin told him only so much, surely he was not going to say he was about to be homeless, because there was nothing any of Justin's family members had wish to or seek to help with, especially not for Justin. They would rather jest or ridicule him about it.

Sixty days was now up and Justin and Shakira had until the next morning to be out. They still had many of their belongings in the duplex. Without a car now, it was hard to move the rest of their minor furniture, but they were going to try to make the effort. Justin and Shakira were outside on the porch trying to gather their thoughts as to what to do next. When a White Tundra truck pulled up, a woman climbed down from the cab, she was short and petite, you could tell that she was an older woman; but her skin was as youthful as a thirty year old, well maintained from head to toe. She came from around the end of the truck, Justin recognized Ms. Deaton right off; Ms. Deaton was a friend of his moms'. Ms. Deaton walked up the walkway where Justin and Shakira were standing; she threw her arms up to wrap them around Justin's neck. She was so happy to see him. She had not seen Justin in a couple of years. Ms. Deaton always felt close to Justin, since she did not have kids of her own and she had always seen something special in Justin.

Ms. Deaton had visited with Justin's mom earlier that day, and she mentioned that she had not heard from Justin in sometime, so Ms. Deaton was not expecting to run into Justin so soon. There was no mention of Shakira either, so she was surprised to learn that Justin was married. Ms. Deaton questioned Justin about him not having contact with his mom. Ms. Deaton was a family person, she believed in the value of family, and although Justin's family was not her blood family, she felt close to them all because she seen them grow up; she has shared memories of the family's good times and difficult times.

Sadly, when she heard what had been happening to Justin and how both sides of the family convicted him she was devastated. Feeling hurt as if this was her own son being falsely accused, she asked what she could do. It did not bother her to interrupt her day, because she knew that she had to help.

Well into the night, they worked diligently to rid the home of their belongings. Ms. Deaton had a truck with an XL cab so they were able to fit in a lot of stuff. The first trip was to the storage. Once Justin and Shakira got back to the house, they realized that it was still a lot of stuff in the duplex and it definitely would not be able to fit in their small storage unit. Shakira asked Ms. Deaton if she knew anyone who could use some household items. She did, and made a quick call from her cell phone that she whipped from the hip pocket of her Gloria Vanderbilt jeans. The call lasted a couple of minutes, and then she turned to Shakira as Justin had just walked up and stood by Shakira. The young girl from her church; Octavia, wants the stuff but was hesitant because she could not spare a lot of money. Ms. Deaton asked Justin and Shakira to let her see what she can get her for eighty dollars. She would pay for it. The three of them entered the garage where Ms. Deaton's eyes set upon a couch set, wood entertainment center, tables, and many other items. She told Justin and Shakira to pick out what they wanted to give up for eighty dollars. They insisted on Ms. Deaton taking whatever she can fit into her truck for last haul; since it was late and everyone was without energy; this had been an all day job of loading and unloading.

With just about everything out of the garage and loaded onto the truck Justin, Shakira and Ms. Deaton headed to Octavia's apartment. Ms. Deaton had called Octavia once they were in front of the gates. There was a brief buzzing, and then the arm of the gate swung back on its hinges to let the truck in. Standing in the doorway of one of the apartments was a young woman, no more than nineteen, or twenty. On her hip was a small child, a girl of ten months and there was two others giggling as they stood in the doorway. The young woman waved her hand in acknowledgement that they were at the right place. Justin and Shakira hopped out the truck and started unloading. It took forty minutes to get everything off the truck and into the apartment. Looking around at her apartment Octavia was grinning from ear to ear. There was a nineteen-inch TV sitting on crates in the living room, and in one of the bedrooms she had a king size mattress on the floor for all of them to sleep. Now she can make her place a home. Octavia turned to the three and could not hold back her tears of joy. She felt that she needed to do something or give more. She was reassured that nothing more was needed. It was a pleasure to help someone in need. Even though Justin and Shakira were in a predicament there selves, they did not solicit anything in return for this gesture of blessing someone who really had appreciation.

Tired and wanting off their feet, Justin, Shakira, and Ms. Deaton jumped into the truck. They stopped off at KFC to grab something to eat and headed home. Ms. Deaton parked her truck in the driveway and turned the ignition off. Shakira offered her to come in the house but Ms. Deaton declined; she did ask what the plans of Justin and Shakira were. There was no plan other than to vacate the premises as promised. Ms. Deaton asked about Shakira's family and if they would be able to stay with any of them. Ms. Deaton could not believe that any member of a family would be so harsh in the event of a mishap to one of their own. Her family was large and somehow they remain civil toward one another and pull together in such times. This is how they stayed afloat for many years. She said that she would be leaving to go back to Louisiana in seven days and if Justin and Shakira wanted to make a change, she would be more than willing to aide them. She would be driving back alone and would love the company; she even stated that she had enough room at home; even for Hadea if she wanted to come. Shakira thanked Ms. Deaton for her genuine kindness and said that they would keep it in mind.

Before the parting of ways, Ms. Deaton wrote down her address in Louisiana and her home number and cell. They had a prepaid cell phone that they planned to keep on for contact purposes and that was the number given to Ms. Deaton. The truck started and Justin and Shakira gratefully thanked Ms. Deaton for stopping her day and helping them, they hopped out of the truck to head inside.

There was still some work to be done before there eviction time, the plan was to eat and relax then get started on what was left to do. There was not much time as it was and they had to be ready at least by 7a.m.; that was only four hours away. Justin and Shakira finished their meal, Shakira threw out the trash and started gathering up everything else that she needed to throw away. The other stuff was going outside on the curb with a "free" sign attached. Justin had fallen asleep in the same spot on the living room floor in which he sat down to eat. Shakira knew that the day before had broke Justin down more so than her. She helped load the truck and unload items too, but some things was too heavy and Justin had to pull a much strenuous load. Shakira worked up to 5a.m., the last thing she remembered was sitting on the bedroom floor closing up the last bag of clothes that was to go with them.

Morning had snuck up on Justin and Shakira. A pounding on the front door jolted the both of them from their sleep. Both of them jumped up at the same time and moved toward the door, bumping into one another Shakira stepped aside and let Justin open the door. He reached for the doorknob to open the front door until he heard "Open up Sheriff's department, Open up"! Justin drew his hand back quickly. At the sound of the next pounding, Justin tells Shakira to hurry and get their things together. Ignoring the pounding and the sound of someone prying open the iron screen door. Shakira headed one way and Justin another to gather the rest of their belongings.

To their acknowledgement, they had only heard the two sets of pounding on the door. However, since the both of them had fallen into a sleep as if it was hibernation time they could not be too sure how long the Sheriff was knocking. They assumed he was out there for some time because now he was adamant about getting in.

Shakira came out the bedroom from gathering up the bags. Just as she took another step the front door was flying open and then a, freeze do not move, followed. Shakira stopped in her tracks, and then she realized that the officer did not see her, he was directing his commands toward Justin. Right behind the officer was a locksmith. He was the one prying open the door for the officer.

Shakira stepped slowly but closer and saw the officer's gun drawn upon Justin. It seemed like a segment taken from the TV show COPS and apparently, the officer thought so too. He came in as if this was a drug bust and not an eviction. Analyzing the way the officer could not conceal his facial expressions well or his body language, meant to Justin that the officer was fresh out of the academy. You could see the intimidation in his eyes even with his gun pointed at Justin. It was no doubt that this officer woke this morning ready to make a name for his self, perhaps to get away from low priority calls such as evictions. By this time the officers' peripheral vision kicked in and he turned quickly and extending his left arm and pointing he commanded Shakira to come out, who are you? The officer asks. In a dry voice, Shakira replied, "I am the tenant of this home". Ignoring her reply, since this information was not what he was looking for. He wanted names and he wanted them at his order. Get over here! Pointing and with authority in his voice, the officer directed Shakira to come where Justin was stranding. Shakira walked over bags still in hand and stood by her husband. The Officer told them to produce their identification; he called it in checking on warrants, his intentions were clear only to him and God. Justin and Shakira only had assumption of the officers' actions so they played it cool.

As they stood there waiting to hear dispatches' findings on them, Shakira thought that it was quite odd that as close as she were standing next to Justin, the gun was not pointed to where it covered both of them, it was pointed only at Justin. The officer was viewing Justin as a threat and not Shakira. Shakira made a mental note to herself to be alert just in case some funny stuff happened. Snapped back from her trance of thoughts she heard dispatch tell the officer that neither of them had warrants. That was the last thing the officer wanted to hear. It was certain that he was looking for some action; at least a scuffle of some sort to make his day.

With much concern as to what Justin and Shakira was doing in the house. In addition, why did they not open the door as instructed? The officer stood with his gun drawn upon Justin; waiting to hear why he ignored his command to open the door. Justin told the officer that they woke up to the pounding and panicked not knowing if there was a chance to get their belongings before leaving. With no response from the officer and a few minutes in passing, Justin started to speak in a emotionless manner as if he was a prey tipping along not to trigger the hunter. "I'm feeling a little uncomfortable and I'm sure my wife is too, you still have your weapon drawn and you see that this has not escalated, clearly this situation is not what you have in mind".

Before answering, the officer moved his head from left to right as if to be loosening up his neck muscles just before a big fight. He held his gun in position a few seconds longer then in a cocky manner the officer withdrew his gun from pointing at Justin and brought it down to be tucked away and resting back on his hip. He says still with cockiness in his reply, "you should've opened the door as I commanded you to and I would not had to pull my gun, you're' lucky I did not think you had a weapon when I came in". After seeing and hearing that, that left Shakira unsettled. She was not only scared, she was also trying to keep herself calm and not have an anxiety attack. Shakira looked over at her husband and saw how calm his demeanor was and that comforted her a tiny bit, but not enough. Her mind started playing out scenarios of the officer being dishonest and trigger-happy. After all, by this time the locksmith was out by his truck piddling around as if to be into getting the things he needed in order to change the locks on the house, while only the officer, Justin and Shakira were the only ones in the house.

Playing in her mind as if she was watching a movie on television, Shakira replayed herself coming out of the bedroom and startling the officer and he shoots her. Alternatively, this officer shooting the both of them and claiming that he felt threatened. Shakira loved watching crime investigations and cop shows just as Justin did, but never did she ever want to be involved in drama of any kind. Shakira always felt like municipal authority was uncompassionate to African American's rights; an immoral she hated to face.

Justin turned to Shakira and says; "Babe you got everything?" Barely getting sound to come out, she answered yeah. Justin tells the officer that he has a bag in the kitchen that he needed and could he retrieve it. The bag was on the counter on the left within arm's reach from where Justin and the officer were standing. Even though this was a house, the layout was small and built on the design of a two-bedroom apartment where the kitchen/dining room area were connected. At this point, the officer played his part of being the end of a mule. The officer said no rather loud, as if this tickled his fancy to have the authority in adding an explanation to his no. Smirking as if this was game point, the officer remarked, "You shouldna been playing games and opened the door, maybe you would have had a chance to gather what you needed. However, you did not and I do not have to let you get anything else. In fact, you don't have any more time to be in here. So come on you need to go, if you remain on the property any longer, you will go to jail for trespassing". It was unbelievable to Shakira and Justin that the officer was still pissed off from his orders ignored.

This was definitely a surreal moment for Justin and Shakira. Everything seemed to have taken place in slow motion. Shakira for one was going through a world wind of emotions. She did not know if she should cry, get angry, or plead for the officer to change his mind.

Seventeen minutes later, they were standing on the street corner with a suitcase, an athletic gym bag, and a shoulder bag. Shakira was delusional; it disturbed her how in a matter of minutes she and Justin were out on the streets. No longer did they have a place to call home, they had just hit the bottom. There they were, standing on the street corner with bags and nowhere to go. Even still, Justin and Shakira were trying to shake the disbelief of how everything just went down. At that moment, Shakira remembered that she left her purse inside the house. Bags and all she ran back down the street. The locksmith was just finishing up and the officer was standing on the front porch. Out of breathe she told the officer that her purse was left inside. Unfazed the officer told Shakira that this is no longer her residents, she was now a trespasser; Shakira had to ask on more time. Can you get it for me; my purse is propped against the wall. Again the answer was no. This time the officer added in something new. He told Shakira that if she did not leave now she would be heading for jail. By this time, Justin had arrived and Shakira told him that the officer was refusing to let her get her purse.

She was dumbfounded. She wondered now, who was playing games. This man in a uniform was denying her of retrieving her purse. In which he had to know she had no identification on her. When he asked for the identification earlier, she took her identification out of her wallet and when he gave it back, she returned it to her wallet and laid her purse against the wall where he had them standing.

Under these circumstances, Shakira pleaded one more time and the officer's response was, "Are you deaf or do you really want to go to jail?" At that moment, she wanted to curse him out, but instead opted to humbly walk away and cuss him under her breath. Justin did not push the issue with the officer; he motioned for Shakira to come back to the bus stop where he was.

Walking again toward the main road where they decided to catch the bus to the storage unit to drop off some of the bags they had. Shakira saw her mom and Hadea driving down the street. Her mom should have thought that it was strange that they were out there that early and with bags. Unfortunately, her good will in dealing with her daughter and son-in-law must have been long gone.

Shakira paid no mind to her mom and her early morning hatred, Shakira's mind was on one thing and one thing only, "her purse". Shakira's first mind was to wait until nightfall and go get her purse out the house, but of course, it was just a thought, the idea of going to jail for breaking and entering was still fresh in Shakira's mind, which had changed her mind about sneaking through the garage backdoor. Not to mention, Shakira remembered that the locksmith had changed all the locks.

More than a few hours went by when Shakira realize that she had no money to go get a new ID, this frustrated Shakira. Again, Shakira started thinking like a criminal, talking hostile and making no sense; saying that she would climb in through the bathroom window, which was sure to be open. Shakira had remembered she removed the stick from the windows track and the window did not have a lock on it, and it would just slide open. Shakira figure she could just climb in if she could get the boost she needed, because the window was too high for her to reach. Justin was still trying to keep humor as he always had done in comical situations. He told Shakira jokingly, "Now you know you can't be in jail." She gave him a little smirk and left it alone, even though she was still thinking about how to report the officer and get her purse. Justin had suggested they call the property manger, but he had been a jerk since he took them to court for nonpayment of rent. He was a slumlord who never kept his word about fixing things. Shakira and Justin proved themselves smarter than he thought. They knew the legal loopholes in the rental agreement and in the tenant rights handbook is where they found solace. The property manager had violated their rights as tenants.

Justin and Shakira made it to the corner. They decided that it was best to head to the storage first and drop off what they did not need to carry with. They had to catch the bus so they went into the store to get change for the bus. Having had to catch the bus after they sold the SUV, they had already accumulated all the main bus schedules. As they walked over to the bus stop that was in front of the store near the street, Justin was already digging for the pack of schedules that he kept rubber band together. He found the one he needed as he dropped his bag down on a cement block that looked as if it was once the base of a payphone. Shakira sat herself down beside the bag on the same cement block. Babe, the next bus is in an hour, Justin tells Shakira. It is not like there was an option; begrudgingly Shakira said all right and moved the bag to make room for Justin to sit.

Talking and thinking about how both sides of the family knew they were going through a hardship and everyone acted as if Shakira and Justin contracted the plague. No doubt each one of the family members were scared that they were going to be the chosen to help. Justin and Shakira never once discussed on which family member they were going to call on for help. They both knew that it was going to be just the two of them going through this, because they believed it to be a spiritual explanation of their destiny. Therefore, neither Justin nor Shakira waited or longed for the aid of family.

Justin and Shakira just could not believe it came down to them being homeless. They were working people. They paid taxes. In addition, they looked for no short cuts or handouts. However, after the business took a fall, figuratively speaking they robbed Peter to pay Paul.

INTENSE SURVIVAL

It was not the plan to start spending any money right away, but Justin and Shakira found a rundown kitchenette that was in the process of being close down. They were walking to nowhere and seen the sign that read "$99.00 a week", they went in and that's when they were told that the city was shutting it down in ninety days, however they could still operate and occupy the premises providing the occupants agree and sign a safety disclaimer. It had something to do with the motel owners not having insurance to cover anyone or thing if something should happen on their premises. The motel housed women of the night and their Jons, right along with other elements of the night. It was as Los Angeles's Sunset Boulevard at its finest.

Now that the housing situation was temporarily under control, Justin and Shakira woke up every morning at 5 a.m. to start walking to that day's destination.

It took them a whole thirty days just to get General Assistance in the sum of $325.00 a month for the both of them and $140 a month for food stamps. In return for the help Justin and Shakira received from the county, they had to attend a work workshop for eight hours a day for two weeks. In comparison to the others, they had to attended class with, Justin and Shakira had the most education and work experience with degrees to back it up. They almost did not comply with the class participation for fear of someone taking it as a gloating session of what Justin and Shakira had previously accomplished. The class was a probation recommendation for drug addicts, an employment program for others made to get off their tails and work for the help they received, and then, it was Justin and Shakira, two people down on luck that could not fight the economic crunch any longer.

Dealing with the county was a headache within itself. So many people have worked the system, and by the time those who really need the assistance, they got the run and was having to jump through hoops for it. Although Justin and Shakira were standing as a married couple some of the breaks where available to Shakira and not to Justin. The system definitely showed favoritism toward women.

Together they never did get help with housing, Shakira had an opportunity for a bed at the women shelter downtown, but she refused. The shelter for men was booked up at least for another two months. The worker on their case looked at Shakira with a puzzled facial expression as she declined the offer to take the bed at the shelter. It was not that serious to be away from Justin in some strange place, while he fended for himself on the streets. The worker looked at Shakira as if she was crazy for making the decision to remain on the streets with her husband. The worker then stated to Shakira that she could not reapply for housing for thirty days. Shakira's decision was final but here was Ms. County worker still trying to convince Shakira to consider the shelter as if she was getting a commission from placing another homeless person. Before the woman spoke another word, Shakira jumped in, thanked her for her time, and then quickly left out of her office.

By the time the workshop ended, Justin and Shakira were no more knowledgeable on resumes, interviews, and appearance then when they first started. Nevertheless, it was over with and now their days begin to fill up with real productivity for themselves.

Eventually, Justin and Shakira left the seedy kitchenette. It was unknowingly as to where they would be at night. More money was going out than coming in which lead to sacrifices. Justin and Shakira spent most of their days at the library. During the night, they would be wonderers of the streets, catching the light rail train in one direction and returning from the other direction.

Justin and Shakira were not in the best of positions but no one can say that they were seen looking down and out. High spirits and faith kept Justin and Shakira going and this was what puzzled their family. They did not know if Justin and Shakira were lying about being homeless, because being homeless meant walking around depressed and looking dirty but that was not the case at all for Justin and Shakira. They were just happy to have each other for moral and spiritual support.

Justin's side of the family knew him as always having a stash of money, so they were in disbelief that he was homeless and broke. Shakira's family knew her to keep a job and a roof over her and provide for Hadea; so they too were wondering what was really going on.

The few friends and family members' houses that Justin and Shakira did go to was short lived. Food was offered, occasional shower, and a good night's rest, after awhile some of Justin and Shakira's friends and family members true colors began to surface. Justin and Shakira decided to stay away before any more harsh feelings begin to rise.

From the college in which Justin graduated, he still had the use of its facilities, so Justin and Shakira used them when needed. They each took showers using the women and men's gym during its least active hours. Every few days Justin and Shakira would go to the 98-cent store and buy a liter of water, one loaf of bread, one pack of luncheon meat, and a large bag of chips. Justin and Shakira would then go somewhere where they could sit, and together they would assemble sandwiches and put them back into the bread bag, making it easier to just grab a sandwich ready made, rather than make them on the go. They were still true coffee drinkers; often they had their own instant coffee with them. All they needed was the hot water and most of the time that was easy to get unless they ran across a penny pinching store clerk who wanted to charge them for hot water to put into *their own* cups.

Some days Justin and Shakira would talk about how they both felt pushed into an experimental project to see how they would survive and react to intense survival. Justin adapted to his new lifestyle. However, this was nothing he wished for his wife to endure; she was trying to stay strong.

Some nights were cold; they had jackets in the storage that they pulled out. Sometimes, even with hats, extra layers of clothing and gloves just would not keep out Mother Natures chill. Justin and Shakira appreciated clear calm nights of 68 degrees.

The experiences of sleeping under the stars was both adventurous and scary for Shakira, this is what took her mind away from reality. One night while walking blocks and blocks to nowhere, looking for an inconspicuous place in hopes of resting their feet and possibly getting some sleep, Justin spotted a vacant parking structure that was very dark in most of the areas of the structure. They walked in with Justin leading the way as Shakira held on to his arm. They found the perfect corner. It was neither wet, nor dirty, and the ammonia that wreaked the place from people using it as a public restroom was gone. Shakira took a navy blue and white travel blanket from the backpack she carried and laid it on the ground. Inspecting their public bedroom once more for anything nasty lying near or critters scurrying, they both sat down. Justin sat with his back against the wall and Shakira sat between his legs. They had found that that way was the best way to keep warmth between them and move quickly if needed. No sooner had they settled in, Justin heard something, a shuffle of some kind. Justin nudged Shakira to get up, as she slowly raised Justin shadowed her. Justin's first thought was rats, but then he focused his sight in on the corners of the structure and seen the stubborn stragglers. Kneeling down to pick up the travel blanket Justin handed Shakira the backpack and he grabbed the other bag and took her hand to lead her out the structure. Neither said a word until they reached the sidewalk. Justin then told Shakira that there was at least two to four other homeless people in the other dark corners, he said one of which was standing urinating. Squatters' rights on the streets and rules among the homeless were not something that was familiar to Justin or Shakira. Whatever the case was, they had no problem leaving the structure. Shakira was glad that Justin did not tell her until afterwards, situations like that, although adventurous, would send her into a mind freeze of panic and blankness.

Just a few blocks down, they found a spot by an office building with three feet high manicured bushes that discreetly hide a small piece of cement walkway that they used to lay their bags on. There was still enough space for Justin and Shakira to sit or lay down as they pleased. Behind a nearby dumpster, Justin found some boxes of various sizes and begins breaking down one to fit the space they were occupying. Once again, they were ready to rest. They ate a sandwich, stretched out on their makeshift pallet. Shakira was lying in front of Justin as they both fell fast asleep.

They took up residency there for a few nights. Always arriving no earlier than midnight, and leaving no later than 5 a.m. Except on Saturday and Sunday when the business was closed they was able to leave at 6 a.m.

Winter was settling in, many of the days were wet and gloomy, and the nights had an ice chill floating in the air. Justin and Shakira's days had been long and drawn out. Still there were no job offers for either of them. Occasionally they would see or talk to one of the family members on Justin's side; it was nothing more than that; a brief hello and a see you later.

After making it to their nightly getaway, the both of them fell fast asleep. Physically and mentally whipped, either one of their eternal clocks alerted them to wake up promptly one weekday morning. Shakira was dreaming that she was running, but her legs were heavy and she felt cold. Coming out of her sleep, she realized that she was cold and her legs were heavy, but she was not running. It had started raining sometime during the early morning hours and since she slept in front of Justin, she was the one graced with the tears falling from the sky. Rocking her body back into Justin to wake him, Shakira realized that they overslept. Employees had started arriving and the parking lot nearly filled with cars less than twenty minutes. Instantly she got up, just as Justin did and they gathered their things without calling too much attention to theirselves and headed for the light rail station, which was a block away. They made it to the light rail station just minutes before the train pulled up that they needed to catch. They both stepped onto the platform and into the train. Shakira had to be wet for another hour, which is how long it took to get to the storage. She was uncomfortable from the wetness of her soaked jeans and the bitter taste in her mouth from last night's food made her stomach turn. Taking their seats, Shakira gave a resting place to their bags; her seat   she felt better leaning against the window, at least until she tires from standing.

TO REBUILD

One day while hanging out at the storage unit eating lunch and trying to regain a piece of mind, Justin and Shakira was trying to figure out what can be done to keep up temporary living quarters with at least a roof and some walls. It just was not making sense to pay out $250.00 for seven days stay at a motel. Justin and Shakira left the option of shelters out all together.

Justin went to throw away the garbage from the lunch they just had. While he was gone, Shakira started repacking the bags and rambling through boxes to get clean clothes and whatever else, they needed. Shakira was so into what she was doing she did not notice that Justin had been gone a little longer than the expected time it takes to reach the garbage and come back. She walked down to the corner of the building but did not see Justin anywhere. As she walked back down towards the storage unit, she saw Justin coming out the storage facilities office. He walked up to Shakira cheesing like a Chest shire cat. She could not wait to see why Justin was so happy. Justin finally spilled the beans, "Shakira, tonight we will be in a larger storage unit, warm, to ourselves and able to sleep without having one eye open!" Shakira with excitement and no questions was now all smiles like her husband.

That night they sat drinking coffee and sharing a package of Turtles candies, when Justin told Shakira how they had been so lucky to acquire the first large storage unit that came open. It turns out that the manager; Hassan had been seeing them come in and out the gates several times a week and then leaving with bags walking. When he saw Justin at the garbage and they began to talk. Eventually, it came around that they were homeless and was trying to get back on their feet. That is when Hassan let the cat out the bag about the "secret community" at the storage facility. He said we could use one of the larger units that was empty, but with some conditions. That was; keep down on the noise, no trash left behind and be in before the security gates close, which was at ten at night. Using the gate code anytime after that would not work because there would be no power to the gate until 7 a.m. the next business day. He also stated to Justin that if for some reason they needed to go out after this time, they would need to stay out of the facility until the next morning.

This aid looked to be a blessing. Justin agreed but did warn Shakira that something was not right about Hassan, and maybe he was wrong, but told Shakira to be careful if he should ever try to approach her while they were not together.

Over the next few days of staying in the unit, they were able to focus on getting back on their feet. Their objective in life was never lost, the worry of having somewhere to sleep other than outside is what kept their objective and goals on the back burner.

Justin and Shakira found a clean pillow top mattress that someone had left in one of the units, and moved it in the unit they slept in, along with some added cover they had packed away; they now had a decent place to sleep at night.

Justin and Shakira finally had the opportunity of seeing a few others getting a breath of air on the grounds of the storage facility after business hours. There was one person who had been living in his unit for three years. He had a job and a car. There was a female, whom they proposed to be "a woman of the night". Justin and Shakira never saw her until night fell when she would be leaving all dolled up as if she were going to a dance.

Knowingly, one mess up could cause everyone to have to adjust their arrangements if there should be any problems that would call attention to the facility, so there were not any problems. That is until the manager himself let his drug habit out the bag. One night, Hassan got some bad dope, he stripped totally naked and armed with his gun he was running around the lot shooting and screaming that the zombies were after him. The business next door was an Asian restaurant that turned into a club afterhour, and one of the patrons called the police. Thank God, Justin had the foresight to have them ready to move from the unit that night. Justin had been feeling uneasy that day as they sat in the unit, at the time he did not know why. When the police came, they did not find zombies but they did find a few people sleeping in the units. The manger asked the officers to check on some of the units because he had heard noises. They started checking the units he was pointing out, which just so happened to be the units occupied by none other than some of the people he allowed to use them; and when they were found the manager denied knowing they were in the unit and they were slapped with a trespassing summons and escorted off the premises.

Justin and Shakira had already moved to an empty unit around the bend staying out of sight of all the commotion. If needed they were able to make an escape. After the commotion had died down, Justin and Shakira begin talking about how lucky they were, because none of the officers seen them. This gave Justin and Shakira an unsettled feeling so they both decided not to sleep there. The first chance they had, Justin and Shakira left the storage facility. Up to this point Justin and Shakira had spent their cash wisely and with income coming in a few days they agreed to find a hotel to get some sleep, and start a fresh new day.

Justin and Shakira stayed away for a few days, before they returned to the storage facility. To their surprise, Hassan the storage manager was still there. Neither Justin nor Shakira was expecting to see him again. Turns out that his parents were the owners of the storage facility, they knew Hassan had an off and on drug problem but thought if he stayed busy he would focus on work rather than drugs. At least this is the story Big John had told Justin. He had been around for the last three years and when he was on the road, he had seen and heard a lot from Hassan and his drug binges. Big John had a million stories to tell about Hassan's drug episodes. Perhaps this was the feeling Justin had once told Shakira he felt about Hassan.

A few months back while at the library Shakira had filled out several job applications online and finally got a call back. The purpose of maintaining the prepaid cell phone account had paid off. Shakira received a message on the phone offering her a position at a furniture store making $10.75 for the first two weeks of training and then commission after that. Although Shakira did not like the idea of a commission job, she did take it. She figured she would try it. Besides, it was across the street from the storage facility where they were staying and all she had to do was walk across the street. She was happy the first week, and then it went downhill from there. Shakira knew her and Justin needed the money, but Shakira hated that job convincingly. It was boring, and Shakira was use to being busy while at work. Some would jump at the opportunity to get no hassles about standing around or sitting waiting on customers, but this was not for her. She worked four twelve hour days and one five-hour day. She sold one bedroom set, her commission was five hundred and sixty dollars; however, another worker who had help close the deal, got a split of the commission.

Shakira spent a lot of her time chatting with the other workers or just walking around looking at the furniture and home accessories; fantasizing of decorating her own home with what she saw. The days were long; most of the time there were no customers for Shakira to pitch the store's bargains. Nearing the end of her guaranteed pay Shakira talked to Justin about quitting her job. In full support of Shakira's decision Justin told her they would take care of it in the morning. Morning came and Shakira was at the doors of her soon to be x-job. Her manager tried to persuade her to stay and give it time, have patients. That was easy for him to say, he had a home, and he had luxuries and convenience. She stood firm, declined, and asked about her check. She had to go through the ringer to get her check but it was worth it, that lump sum of money helped tremendously to carry Justin and Shakira over. The search for a job was on again, and it was not long before an opportunity was knocking once more.

They had picked up a flier one day at one of the food banks where they frequently went to get a hot meal. It was about a help center that offered free use of the computer, phones and aid for help in job placement. This was the next place to check out. Located downtown; and not in the good area of downtown is where they found the career center. As Justin and Shakira rounded the corner of the building, they came to a line of people waiting outside the doors. They moved to the front of the building and of course, the front of the line. Some of the people in line directed remarks toward them. However, Justin and Shakira ignored them and kept moving. They rung the bell of the office door and a woman came to the door and hollered through the glass that they do not open until 1:00 p.m., which was five minutes away. Gesturing okay with a nod of his head Justin stepped back and waited for the doors to open. It was not until later Justin and Shakira found out why those remarks were directed toward them as they were walking up to the front of the line. This office offered much more help than they knew of; and the services were all free. They gave lunch vouchers, gas vouchers, paid for you to get identification and birth certificates. Unfortunately, it was all on a first come first serve basis. Justin and Shakira now understood why those folks in line felt as though they were trying to bow guard their way in. Again, Justin and Shakira were right in the mist of ex offenders, drug users and all other kinds of street elements that formerly they would not be in the same company of.

Upon entering, they stopped at the front desk and asked where the job center was. One of the volunteer workers directed Justin and Shakira to go around the corner. As Justin and Shakira entered the doorway, it was expected to be a full room, but as many people as it was outside lined up for free commodities, there was only two that made it to the job center. The director of the program greeted them. Mrs. Leann; she was a husky woman in her early sixties. She had a Caribbean accent that complimented her genuine spirit. In fact, she became quite comfortable with Justin and Shakira during their every day visits to the center. Mrs. Leann was always kind to them. She spent time after the center closed and would talk with them, sometimes even sharing her lunch with them. She learned more about their situation and even a little of who they were. Mrs. Leann knew the qualities of Justin and Shakira; it was something powerful and pure. It became a joy to Mrs. Leann seeing Justin and Shakira. Captivated, Mrs. Leann went out her way to help Justin and Shakira the best she could. Before a months ending, Justin and Shakira had became more than clients of the help center; Justin had taken up helping some of the other clients with resumes, computer help or shooting the breeze with other helpful, informative tips. Shakira let Justin have this pleasure; she was not much of a people person as Justin was. Therefore, she used this time to catch up on emails and job follow-ups for herself and Justin.

For two months straight, rain and cold Justin and Shakira never missed a day going to the help center. Both of them were on top of revising and posting their resumes daily. They participated in mock interviews at the help center, and Mrs. Leann would get job postings that she normally posted on Mondays, and the one's she thought would interest Justin or Shakira, she would already have them put aside for when they arrived. The efforts were great, but nothing panned out for either Justin or Shakira. Mrs. Leann gave Justin and Shakira a heads up on a lead for open positions at a new Goodwill drop center, which was soon to be opening. She told them the center would be having on the spot interviews. So the day the interviews, Justin and Shakira made sure they got to the center early. A woman by the name Ms. Davis was conducting the interviews; she was also the hiring coordinator at the Goodwill. She came strolling in promptly at 11 a.m., with a greasy look to her face as if it was triple degree weather and she was beginning to melt. Shakira dismissively assumed that it was because of all that cheap oily orange foundation she had applied so heavily to her face and neck. Her Ruby Red #78 gloss had brought attention to her already voluptuous lips and made them look as though someone had swatted her right in the kisser.

It was five in attendance all together; it was a group interview. During the interview process, Ms. Davis talked to the group as a whole then one by one. The other three people left immediately after their interview; Justin and Shakira stayed behind as they usually did. At least until it closed, which was at 1:00 p.m.

Justin and Shakira were side by side, both on a computer checking their emails, when Ms. Davis came over and commented on each of their skills and work experience; as seen on their resumes. She sat down alongside them and began asking how interested they were in the positions at the Goodwill. She told them the location again, as she did during the interview earlier, and asked if transportation would be a problem. Knowing they did not have a car Justin and Shakira were both on the same page in answering her question, remembering where she said the location was, and knowing the area, they insinuated as though they had a place nearby. It was great getting a chance to talk in depth more about the position. There was no doubt either Justin or Shakira had an opportunity of being offered a job.

Suspiciously, Ms. Davis started directing her attention to Justin more; it was at that time Justin recognized she was an instrument of destruction. She stated how impressive it was that Justin held a degree. She almost seemed shocked, and then to listen to a well-spoken, well-mannered male that showed humility and meekness made her skeptical. She had to have thought one or two things; he was a slick man that fabricated his education and work experience or he was investigating her work ethic. Some of her questions started teetering on the line of being critical. Justin and Shakira could not believe how this turned all of a sudden. Nevertheless, Justin remained unmoved by Ms. Davis' intentions, while Shakira was getting bothered. In a matter of minutes, it turned from professional and into a personal battle of the wits. Whatever it was about Justin, Ms. Davis wanted to tear it down.

She started asking Justin if he considered working construction, she could start him working that week. She even told him that she had contacts for the State Fair. She did not see any construction positions at all on Justin's resume, no labor work of any kind, for that matter. What she did see blindly was; Managerial positions at business offices, Accounting, and then his degree in Criminal Justice, along with credentials in Commercial Music. Ms Davis tried and tried in complete disorder to stir Justin up. It was comical for Justin; he rather enjoyed it.

It was time to shut this woman up, Shakira thought. No longer was she going to remain silent and let this woman try to work her black magic of destruction. She just did not know what she was up against trying to belittle Justin. Nevertheless, she did not need to hear ammunition of curse words, what she needed was a tongue lashing from a spiritually deep-rooted person. Shakira sat back and waited for her king to verbally attack. She knew Justin could handle this woman and make her think about her intentions for days to come. When it came, Justin did it in such a calm diplomatic manner that Ms. Davis knew at that time that she possibly jumped in blind on this one. She turned on her heels so quick and tried to escape out of there as promptly as she entered.

All the while Mrs. Leann was sitting on the other side of the table with a little smirk on her face. She knew this woman's game just as well as Justin did.

Then it was over, nothing stated about a job, or a phone call for a job, just the essence left behind of Ms. Davis' Chantilly perfume.

Even after that crazy stunt by Ms. Davis, that did not detour Justin or Shakira from what they needed to gain. They still went to the help center and eventually it started to pay off. They end up signing up for a free training class for the retail industry. It was a six-week course with an internship and possible permanent hire on with one of the retailers that took part in this program. At this point, they were up for anything. The help from the county was running out. Living like this was out of the ordinary for them and it was starting to wear them down.

Class started and the first day of class seemed promising enough, that they continued going. Justin and Shakira found themselves misplaced in a class among beginner job seekers and people with little experience. It was the easiest way at the time to get a foot in the door working steady, so they had to bear with it.

The instructor was an older petite woman named, Ms. Bannon. She was very well dressed, and resembled Jamie Lee Curtis, she spoke very proper; as if she had been a librarian or an English teacher at some point.

Through the course of the class, Justin and Shakira relearned resumes, and more steps to guide you through an interview. After going over both of their resumes, Ms. Bannon had suggested that both Justin and Shakira revise them. Given the experience and credentials they had, Ms.

Bannon had told them that their resumes were a little intimidating for a minimum wage position. They did revise their resumes and by the fifth week, they were ready to start picking an employer to apply for internships with. In the process of Justin waiting to hear back from the employer that last interviewed him, an internship came through for Shakira at one of the largest clothing retail chains in America. She knew that if she just got her foot in the door than everything else would fall into place.

OFF TRACK

Shakira was living in a world of fantasy. Living on the streets was baring a burden on her. There was times when she would be very angry with Justin. She was missing Hadea, missing her mom and above all a place to call home. She had dropped from 125lbs down to 109lbs. Since her frame was small, this much of a weight loss was not a good look for her. Shakira's skin was dull; there was not even a sparkle in her eyes when she smiled. Justin as well, was taking a mental beating each day his wife blamed him, each day that she would act as if she was losing her mind, and each day that he had prayed. He too looked as if he carried the weight of the world on his shoulders. His weight too, had plummeted, but for Justin it was a plus; he had some extra pounds that he needed to lose.

He was happy that doors started opening for them. There was no doubt in his mind that Shakira would be permanent on her position. However, as a man he had to make something happen for them. One day he thought he had the answer to what he was looking for. This particular day was one of Shakira's off days. She had been picking at Justin over nothing all day long. Justin eventually fell into Shakira's web of the bickering battle. Back and forth, they went with angered words, and by the time, they had reached their stop to get off the bus Justin had had enough. He exited the bus with his feet already in motion to carry him quickly away from Shakira's mouth. She threatened behind him that she was going to her moms' house. Ignoring her all the way Justin went through the gates at the storage facility. Feeling defeated and angry, Shakira turned around and went across the street to IHOP, she figured that if Justin wanted to eat he would come to her, since she had the debit card. Justin made it to the storage unit and opened the lock with his key. He had rigged a latch that would pull the door shut from the inside so he could lock it from inside. He sat down on the mattress laid back and pulled out his phone. He was sitting there thinking how foolish Shakira was acting. Justin had encouraged Shakira weeks ago to go to her mom's house and be with Hadea; but Shakira was stubborn and to proud at the time, he knew Shakira needed to go to her moms and be with Hadea and he could not forcibly make her go.

Through out the years Justin kept in contact with his childhood friend Devon. They met when they were twelve and fourteen. While lying there he remembered that Devon left a voice message for him a couple of days ago. Justin sat up with his back against the storage unit's cold steel wall, Justin scrolled through his phone until he found Devon's number. Justin pressed the call button, instantly connecting to a ringing line. By the third ring Devon was picking up the phone, already knowing Justin was on the other end. They had talked for almost two hours straight, catching up on the three years of passing without knowing what the other was doing. It was always possible to get a hold of one another through the many mutual friends in common, so a number was always simple to get, if there was one. They each shared what they have been doing and what is going on now in their lives. Hearing that Justin was in a predicament, Devon suggested that Justin come down to where he lives and try to establish his self there. Justin considered saying yes at that very moment; but he had to consider his wife. She just started her internship and he wanted her to stay focused and move forward with gaining a position. After toggling thoughts in his mind, Justin told Devon that he would call and confirm with him later with what he was going to do. Just then, Shakira was tapping on the door. Justin got up and let her in without saying a word. Shakira was ashamed for her actions; these were the same actions repeatedly. She slid past Justin and sat on the mattress. She stuck a white Styrofoam plate out and said, "Here". Justin locked the door and turned to get the plate. Justin opened up the lid as he sat back down against the wall, the aroma of a hot Turkey and Swiss sandwich with fresh crisp fries. As Justin sat and ate his meal he thought about the many things he can discuss with Shakira about her actions, but he figured it was no use. He knew that at some point through a calm discussion Shakira's defense mechanism of hostility would kick in and she would be ready for battle. Therefore, he avoided the matter all together. It was hurtful to know that he would have another opportunity to confront Shakira when she "loses her mind" again. Justin opted to discuss his decisions on relocating to Merced. He told her that she should swallow her pride and go to her mom's apartment. He reminded her of her dedication to get this far after being at the bottom. Shakira refused to go to her moms even though she knew it would be of a great convenience. She wanted to go where Justin went even if it meant giving up her internship and starting over. Justin and Shakira decided that this might be a good lead so they agreed that they would leave later that night. Since it was the weekend, Shakira had until Monday to figure out how she was going to handle the internship. Not having much too up root themselves from, they decided to see if a better opportunity awaited them in Merced. They packed clothes and paperwork. Justin called Devon back to confirm the plans of going to Merced where Devon was.

By the end of the conversation, Devon confirmed that he would pick up Justin and Shakira at 10:00 that night. Devon assured Justin that he and Shakira were more than welcomed to come and stay at Devon's and his girlfriends until they got back on their feet.

Devon arrived right on time as promised. Justin and Shakira were ready to go; they loaded their belongings into the van and hopped in. Devon had his girlfriend and her two grandkids with him. Devon's girlfriend was more like his "sugar momma". Her name was Peaches. She was sixty-eight years old and looked every bit of it. She held close to four hundred and eighty pounds on her five feet four inch structure.

Peaches' seven and twelve year old grandkids appeared to have been well mannered. The drive down took about an hour. Justin and Shakira were well entertained during the ride. They learned that Peaches had somewhat an understanding of God and spirituality. She spoke about people coming into one another's life for a reason and this is what she presumed herself to be in Justin and Shakira's life, a person with a spiritual purpose, which was to help.

They arrived at the house and unloaded the van. Everyone went inside and Justin and Shakira were showed where they could put there things. Devon and Peaches gave Justin and Shakira a few moments to settle in and then they showed them the rest of the house and the hideaway bed in which they would be sleeping on. It was late and the kids had already fallen asleep. Devon and Peaches went upstairs to their room. Justin and Shakira pulled out the sofa bed and were soon fast asleep.

The next morning Justin and Shakira both woke up feeling so refreshed. They took turns taking a long hot shower and getting dressed. By this time, the kids were coming downstairs, still in their pajamas and looking for cereal to eat. Peaches and Devon were up too. Peaches apologized for not having much food in the house, but said she would go shopping today. She did have coffee, that is all Justin and Shakira wanted. The grownups sat around talking. Shakira asked about all the nearby stores, the mall and about how the buses ran.

After a few hours, the women were getting ready to go to the store while leaving the males at home. On the way to the store, Peaches and Shakira talked about various topics. Peaches did most of the talking, being she was well endowed on life's experiences, as she thought.

Arriving at the store Peaches told one of the grandkids to get a basket. She found one of the electric chairs that the stores provide to handicap persons or the elderly. It was hard for Peaches to carry her weight walking long distances. Peaches headed for the home improvement aisles, while Shakira went straight for the food aisle. They had just received their food stamp benefits and had $300.00 on the card. The benefit amount doubled since they completed the class. Shakira had no intentions on spending all of the food stamps but she did make sure that since she and Justin ate no beef or pork she got what they normally ate. Peaches was coming up the aisle with her basket on the electric chair and the shopping cart full of towels, toys, and clothes asked Shakira if she was ready. Shakira had finished shopping; and not minding the basket she saw filled like it was Christmas, she asked Peaches if she needed any food. Shakira stuck her foot in her mouth asking that. Peaches got at least eighty dollars worth of stuff. It would not have been so bad if it were things to make a meal. She had the grandkids loading the basket with soda, chips, candy, and pizza and had the nerve to get a couple of packs of Angus beef patties. Shakira end up spending two hundred dollars from the food stamp benefits. Just as Shakira knew, the items she bought lasted no time, in one week, there was no chips, no candy, and all the soda was gone. Those Angus patties were still in the freezer, but the chicken and turkey bought quickly disappeared. Shakira soon learned that the night at the store, her generosity came as a pleasurable rescue. Peaches spent her money on the luxuries for her home while she let Shakira buy the luxuries of the food. Each grocery trip after that, Peaches bought no soda, no expensive Angus beef patties, in fact she barely bought anything that needed to be cooked. Regularly, after work she bought all kinds of fast food home; from at least three different fast food chains that she had to pass on the way home. Shakira and Justin were not big fans of eating out;

they preferred a home cooked meal, so they went shopping with their selves in mind.

They made sure that they were up early and back late when they left Peaches and Devon's house. Justin and Shakira seem to have covered the entire city applying for positions. Now it was a matter of following up and waiting. It may have appeared to the outside eyes that Justin and Shakira were not handling their business. Peaches started coming home from work with a chip on her shoulder. Her once friendly greeting turned into an Ogre's grunt. In her mind, Justin and Shakira were not doing anything to help *her* situation nor *her* pockets. It was true they did not give her cash in her hand, but her house and dishes was always clean. She did not have to shell out money on any cleaning supplies, paper necessities for her home and any food bought and cooked by Shakira, or Justin was accessible to anyone who wanted to eat some. Sadly, the grandkids were spoiled brats that got anything they wanted. They even wasted a lot of food and this was okay. All this was a shadow over Peaches' eyes. She boasted about being the age she is and still able to work. Her pride was the maintenance of a charity foundation. Peaches always boasted about being trusted by the owner in doing the accounting for the company, the hiring, and overseeing the workflow of the employees. She tried to talk down to Justin and Shakira as if they had no goals, no experience, and claimed that this is why they were in a financial dilemma. Peaches had the nerve. She was not making her living solely on her own. Peaches had a company credit card paid every month by the owner according to her; the owner never views nor did questions the credit cards monthly statements, the owner just sign the checks in approval for payment. She shopped an awful lot, and it was on meaningless splurges for the kids or Devon. It seemed as though she was teetering on the lines of embezzlement. Her claims to and about Justin and Shakira were thoughtless to them. They understood the true character of

Peaches. She controlled Devon. If he made her mad, she would take away the use of the car. She controlled how he spent her money. Devon had no job and the only thing Peaches expected from him was to be with her. Peaches could not control anything with Justin and Shakira. She also hated the fact that they did not need her help other than her hospitality of letting them stay there.

For three weeks, Justin and Shakira endured smudged looks and had even notice how the grandkids stop talking to Justin and Shakira as they use to. They were deciding to leave when they got a call asking them to come in for an interview. The position was for a couple to manage a storage facility. They both would receive $700.00 a week, a two-bedroom apartment rent-free and free cable and internet services. This was great, if they got the position it was to start immediately. The next day they were up early and arrived at the interview. The interview took an hour and a half, because the interview steered in various directions between Justin, Shakira, and the couple interviewing them. By the end of the interview, they were hired. The next step was to be prepared to start work in a week when the apartment was ready. They would have one day to move in and then the next day start work. They arrived back at the house. The kids were home from school; annoying one another as usual. Devon was in the study watching TV. Before anything could come out about the day they had, Devon had said that Peaches was coming home early and wanted to talk to them about paying rent for being there. Justin always leveled with a person and told them straight up how he felt about something he felt was wrong. This was truly wrong. Justin told Devon that he was going on his word that it was fine for them to come, meaning Justin thought Devon talked it over with Peaches. Justin also reminded Devon that he told him there financial situation and only could contribute to food and necessities as they have been doing. Devon stood listening to Justin's words sink in. Devon looked up at

Justin as if a light clicked on in his mind. Devon turned into what seemed like a frightened child that had broke momma's antique vase. He blamed Peaches for her funny ways, he blamed her for trying to break up a lifelong friendship, and at the point of blame Peaches was right on cue with her entrance. She was walking through the garage door that led to the kitchen.

Peaches walked into combat right in her own house because Justin and Shakira had just about enough of this woman thinking she had a superior hand above them. Peaches had received a physical lashing of words, then a spiritual lashing of words. There was no violence, no threats, or anger raised while in conversation. Then the air seemed to have cleared its cloudy layers. However, Justin and Shakira were still mistaking because they were prejudged. Justin and Shakira were counting down the days until they would have killed two birds with one stone. They were able to obtain a job and housing. The next step was to go get Hadea from Nana BG's house.

There was still a chip carried on Peaches' shoulder. She was wondering how much longer she was going to have to put up Justin and Shakira. She had no clue that it would be sooner than she thought. Peaches displayed jealousy toward the time Justin and Devon spent hanging out. Even if Justin and Devon were in the study catching up on old times and laughing, she would be right there wanting in on the conversation. Moreover, wanting to know what was so funny. Peaches and Shakira had often sat in the living room and talked. Regardless of the topic, Peaches managed to turn it in the direction of herself and her grandkids. Shakira knew from times in the past on how to shut Peaches up. Shakira starting getting the feeling Peaches envied her and Justin's marriage. She saw the love and closeness between her and Justin. Peaches wanted the same from Devon. Devon was nothing like Justin. He was an adult who was stuck in his teen years. He talked about Peaches, and her weight, he acted foolish and juvenile. The only thing Devon was serious about was music and at times, he seemed unbalanced in handling that.

Peaches wanted Devon to be devoted to her; unfortunately, Devon's devotion to her was not talking about her in public. In order to make herself feel better she would reminisce about her first marriage. She lightened when she spoke about the love and the bond shared between her and her husband. After losing him to cancer, she had never found anyone else, except for her "boy toy" Devon.

Justin and Shakira were sitting side-by-side on the front porch swing later that night. They had felt the eyes from inside upon them; the standing hairs on back of their necks told it all. Justin's phone rung, it was his mom. He answered with questions already buzzing around in his mind. She had called to say that she was going into the hospital in the morning and she just wanted to tell Justin in case something should happen. Justin sprang up as if he had a pocket full of fire ants. It takes a lot to work Justin up. One thing for sure he does not like to hear that anyone in his family has to go through an ordeal such as surgery. He questioned her as to what was wrong, but she would not say. Justin's mom talked really slow and calm as to imply that this was a serious matter. Justin told her that he was coming from out of town but will be there in a few hours. She unconvincingly told him that he did not have to come. Justin made his mind up right that moment; he knew they needed to leave that night. Hanging up the phone from his mom Justin told Shakira that they were leaving so when they go in start getting their belongings together and he will tell Devon. Shakira was in a panic and did not know what to think what was wrong with her mother in law. Shakira did want to jump out of her skin in excitement to be leaving the discontentment environment that she and Justin was discouraged by. Justin went in and told Devon about his mom and told him asked if he could take them back today.

Justin offered gas money but Devon denied it. He and Justin went back many years and had always been close even if they had lost contact for a time, they would come back together and be as if they never lost touch. Devon was equally hurt to hear that Justin's mom was going into surgery, and he felt for Justin because he saw the pain in his eyes and heard the distraught tone in his voice. It was easy to get everything together. Shakira had kept everything organized and always packed in the closet they used. For one, she liked organizing just about anything; two, she did not doubt for once that Peaches or her grandkids would go rummaging through her and Justin's belongings. If it was a way Shakira left her items, it would be unnoticeable to anyone else that she strategically placed each item in certain positions so she would know right off if their belongings had been tampered with or not.

It was 8:45 p.m., and they were ready. Originally, Peaches and the kids were going to stay home but at the last minute, she wanted to go. Fifteen minutes gone and they were barely leaving the driveway. The girl grandchild forgot her chips on the counter and whined to go and get them. Peaches obliged as if this was more of a pressing issue then the one at hand. For the second time since they had been there, Devon put his pants on and told Peaches that she is holding up everything. He fussed at her for giving in to such a minuet request.

The arguing started and the name-calling came out. Peaches was more embarrassed than anything, she did not say much more after that she just sat the whole way and pouted like a small child.

The kids were sleep when they made it to the storage facility. Devon and Justin got out and unloaded the van. Shakira got out and closed the side door of the van. She stepped over to the passenger window where Peaches was. Shakira felt that Peaches was undeserving of her sincere thank you, but she was not going to let that stop her from doing what was morally right. She told Peaches thank you. The chip fell off Peaches' shoulder; she reached her hand out and wished them well. Now that Shakira was from under her roof, she told Peaches she had mistaken her for a true spiritual person and if she had been, she would have recognized the truth about them, not what she thought or saw. Peaches' mouth gapped open and she grabbed her chest as if to be offended, but no words were able to out. Shakira turned in relief as she passed Devon walking through the hallway that lead to Justin and Shakira's storage unit. Justin was right behind; they were saying their goodbyes and Justin told him that he would call with the news on his mom. Certain, that as soon as Devon was in the van Peaches was telling on Shakira and Shakira was telling Justin what she had said to Peaches.

  Justin opened the lock to the unit and they went in. Having not been there in almost a month it sure did feel good to lay on the mattress and have solitude again. First thing, that morning Shakira called the owner of the storage facility in Merced and apologized for them having to decline the offer of the position. Shakira explained that Justin's mom was going into the hospital and they needed to go back to the city where she resided. The owner was sympathetic and understood. Shakira hung up the phone. Justin tried to call his aunt and got no answer, so he called his other aunt he knew would be home, since she was bound to a wheelchair. She did not have any news to tell, other than she just knew her sister was going into surgery at noon. She did not tell anyone the reason behind the surgery and she started telling only two days ago. Since Justin and Shakira knew, they had some time before Justin's mom went into surgery to head over for breakfast across the street, since the next bus was not coming for another hour. They got breakfast to go and headed to the bus stop.

  They made it to the hospital and went straight to admissions. They found out what room Justin's mom was residing in. Justin asked, "How is my mom doing?" Justin's aunt told him that she was in recovery and had not made it to her room yet. Justin tried getting information on what the problem was, but was unable to get any information, even though it was his mom. The hospital told Justin that his mom requested that they did not release any information about her surgery. Justin was puzzled; all he wanted to do was see his mom. They waited around for almost two hours before they checked to see if she was in her room yet.

Justin's mom arrived to her room; she was still under heavy medication. She woke for a few minutes to acknowledge Justin's presence. She looked over to Shakira and reached for her, Shakira went closer to the bed, lost for words as she grabbed her mother in laws hand. In and out of her drug-induced sleep Justin tried to get information out of his mom, she stayed tight lipped about her surgery. She assured them that she was okay then drifted back in a sleep. Justin and Shakira stayed around a while longer hoping that his mom would wake again but she was out. Justin and Shakira left. The clouds had moved in and it started to rain. Justin and Shakira caught the next bus to head back into shelter at their tin storage home. Justin had felt like the day was unproductive, he found out nothing about his mom. Patience just had to be a virtue until morning when he will try again to gather information on his mom's condition.

Settling back in with sandwiches from Subway and cups of water they sat and talked about time testing them once more. Once more, they planned to push on.

Morning set upon Justin and Shakira and he woke with his mom on his mind. He dialed the hospital and asked for her room number. Justin was connected and by the third ring, his mom's weak voice was on the other end. Justin had a million questions. No straight answers just around the block jargon came from his mom. The only straight answer Justin got was that she was getting out at two that day. Justin asked if he wanted her to go to her house and get it ready for her. His mom said that she had Gary, Justin's' auntie's second boy to Jermaine, and his girlfriend staying at her house and they can get things together. Justin told his mom that he would give her time to rest and visit her when she got home. It was upsetting to hear that his mom did not turn to him for help. She was in preference to letting her nephew and his girlfriend stay in her extra room. She knew Justin and Shakira were homeless and she never offered. Justin was indeed upset but at the same time, he held so much compassion for whatever his mom was going through.

A few days passed before Justin and Shakira popped up at his mom's house. Gary's girlfriend Keysha let them in. Gary was lying in the bed of the extra bedroom; Justin peeked in and said, 'What's up man?" Gary got up from the bed and gave Justin a hug. Shakira moved passed Justin and went toward his mom's room. Her mother in law was in bed. Shakira walked over and gave her a hug. Justin came in right behind Shakira and kissed his mom on the cheek. Asking how she was doing they could not help but notice that she had a smile on her face like she just hit the lotto jackpot. They figured she was happy to be home, they knew how much she hated going to the hospital and having drugs for pain pumped into her. Finally, she asked if she looked any different. Neither Justin nor Shakira had recognized anything different, and then she blurted out that she had undergone a tummy augmentation and a breast lift. Silence filled the room, they were speechless while his mom had no idea how much added stress she had put on Justin. The only thing that came to mind was to tell her how he felt and that he was glad that she was okay. Justin turned to Shakira and asked if she was ready. Out the door, they went and in Justin's mind, he thought about how evil keeps stopping at particular doors using the family as instruments and then keeping each waiting to shine when it becomes their turn.

Nothing further about Justin's mom was said, which Shakira knew best to leave it alone. A sacrifice was made for the sake of family and it turned out to be just a big old' slap in the face again.

Settling back in on the right track Shakira regained her position as an intern. It took her a week and encouragement from Justin to get the nerve to call and talk to the store's manager. She was humble in speaking while she graveled to having a second chance. The retail store accepted Shakira back and gave her two days to be at work. Shakira's mind was finally at ease.

She did not feel like a total failure. Shakira had in mind this time to go through this full force, no stopping and certainly no interruptions. As for Justin, he was hot on the trail of new beginnings and traumatic endings. Out of his circle was his mom. He loved her and could not deny her; even though he knew what sounded good coming from her, was only the devils vail to keep him beneath the pure light that waited to shine on him.

LIAR, LIAR

Things started to look up for Justin and Shakira. Shakira had been on her internship for two months. She was able to make it there as scheduled, and on time. It only called for her to do four hours, and in those four hours, she made sure that it was productive. Shakira's work ethic had always been exceptional, and it soon became recognized with management, which landed Shakira a permanent position with pay. Justin did not hold his breath on hearing back to start an internship so he had started pursuing his entrepreneurial passion. He took his business skills and put them to use.

Justin's mom had called one day and had been calling ever since. After several casual talks, it finally came out to what she wanted. The same with Shakira's mom, she called out the blue one day and invited them over to dinner. From that day and after she had been calling, inviting them over, and accommodating an occasional hot shower.

Justin and Shakira was still living out of the storage facility. Their county money had stopped, but they remained with the food stamps. Justin had picked up some extra cash through his business endeavors. He made a lump sum and was able to get them a car. This made it easier for Justin and Shakira to get around. Seeing that they were getting on their feet little by little, their families were starting to accept them again. Justin and Shakira felt they cured themselves of some sort of social disease.

Out of the two of them, Justin expected that everything and anything kept in the dark would surely come to the light. Untimely it did when things seemed to be looking up for Justin and Shakira. Nevertheless, evil was still lurking. The reason Shakira's mom had been having them over was because she was losing control of Hadea. Hadea had became hostile and belligerent towards Nana

BG. Nana BG thought that if Shakira were to come around more than Hadea would not act out as much. Shakira quickly found out why Hadea's attitude had shifted into overdrive. Her grades and GPA fell tremendously. She was good at covering her tracks and keeping it away from Nana BG. Not to mention she was involved with a boy. For days, Hadea had been manipulating her time, cutting class, and missing her curfew to be with her new boy friend. Her anger and tolerance for being around Nana BG had flourished into a rage of horror.

Justin's mom was going into surgery in about a week for her back. This time she told Justin straight out, she's tired of Justin closing her out of his life for her actions.

Her recovery would be at home, only if she had a caregiver. The caregiver would be of her choice and it could be family. So when she extended the offer for Justin to be her caregiver, he accepted. It was the understanding that she would pay Justin in return for running errands, cleaning and whatever else she needed. Although the extra money would be great to have, Justin would have helped his mom free. Her surgery had gone well and now she just needed the recovery time. Justin's time changed instantly with errands, some of which, was of pure nonsense, but he completed them anyway. He cooked meals, and even went to fast food places in order to sustain his mom's taste for the foods liked. When Justin's mom was able to move around more, she took to having him drive her around to different places at least four times out of the week. Sometimes Shakira would have to wait after work for Justin to come get her, knowing that Justin's mom was milking him for every minute plus more. Unfortunately, the arrangement agreed upon between Justin and his mom was for her gain. The complaints had started to come. His mom had a complaint for just about everything Justin did for her. Any meal Justin prepared, his mom would complain that he did something wrong. Instead, he got another complaint. She complained that when she sent him to get her some takeout food that it is not correctly cooked, and he would take it back as she requested him to do so.

To make sure he received his pay on time Justin had been making sure to fill out his time sheet and drop it off on time. However, he had yet to receive any money and it was going on his third time sheet. He asked his mom about the check and she assured him that the office was slow in cutting the checks. She freely grabbed her purse and handed Justin a hundred dollar bill. Justin did not want to take money from his moms' pocket; but she insisted and said that she knew he had been helping her and she appreciated it. Justin and his mom did not share moment like this often; it made Justin forget about the past resentment. Justin told his mom that when he get a check cut to him for his services than he would give it back to her. Justin had some time before picking up Shakira and decided to go to the office that hosted the caregiver services. What he found out nearly knocked him to the floor like a boxers blow making contact with him. Justin's mom had requested that the checks come to her address and in her name since she was the "requester". This was something that could be done it just was not expected, Justin's mom maliciously did not discuss any such part of this change with him.

Once more, Justin had nothing but questions as to how can a mother handle her child in such a disruptive manner. She seemed like she did not want to see him succeed in life. She denied the fact that she had a son whose level of intelligence far exceeded the average person. Justin did not adhere to what she wanted him to do; she built a wall against anything he pursued. Justin told Shakira it has been that way for years and it is still that way. Maybe she was frightened that she would not vast in his glory or would not be able to gain something from Justin's success, therefore she was working on pushing herself away.

Justin had conversations in the past with his mom, but her mentality about Justin's heartfelt, deep-rooted conversations was as foolishness, she laughed at his thoughts, his theories, and his wisdom of spirituality. Justin's mom was confused; she did not see Justin as a spiritual person; but as a religious person, which lead her to misjudge her own son. Therefore, when he spoke of his Father she denied his knowledge and guidance. She was a strong woman, however too strong, she was the parent, and as an adult, she wanted Justin to acknowledge that he was to listen to her, not her listen to him. This was definitely a conflict in itself; Justin's mom played the inferior/superior game to see how hard Justin would fall.

Shakira worked the morning shift, so she was off at three. Justin was waiting in the car outside the store when Shakira walked to the car and got in; she leaned over and gave Justin a kiss. Shakira buckled up her seat belt and before they were out the parking lot, she was already telling Justin about the day she had had and the customers she had dealt with. Justin loved to see his wife happy; she even started to get her spark back in her eyes and the glow back to her skin. Shakira finally ran out of stories to tell and asked Justin how his day went. After hearing all that Justin went through again with his mom, she sympathized with her husband. Shakira saw the times Justin had bent over backwards to accommodate some of his moms even most ridiculous requests. Shakira had thought back to over the years, how her mother in law although pleasant in meeting; she held an envious streak to Shakira's marriage to her son. She had begun to feel as though Shakira was unworthy of Justin for letting her family treat Justin as they did. Who was she to determine Shakira's worthiness of Justin? This problem was with all the family who was persistent on pushing Shakira and Justin apart. They were trying to stop what God had planned, and no one was a true host of God on either side of the family, the understanding of what God says and about the laws of marriage. Everything was by sight, not by faith.

Shakira came out of thought when she noticed they were heading in the direction of her moms house. It was then Justin told her that her mom called and left a voicemail saying come for dinner; she needs to talk to them. Shakira tensed up, thinking what now. She had no idea what was up her moms' sleeve. They arrived at Nana BG's house and parked. They both walked up to the front door they were walking the Green Mile. Making to the front door Shakira knocked. The smell of hot fried chicken filled the air. Shakira heard her mom call out that the door was open; she turned the knob and opened the door. The aroma of biscuits, vegetables, and apple pie hit Justin and Shakira in the face like a fresh spring breeze. Hadea had not made it from school, but was due in soon. Shakira's mom had made plates of food for Shakira and Justin. Shakira's mom wasted no time in spilling the beans about what Hadea had been doing. Hadea was out of control, she had possessed a mouth of an exorcist against her Nana BG. They were in constant verbal battle each night.

Shakira's mom suspected that Hadea was sweet on the older man who lived in the same townhome community, two doors down. She could tell something was up between the two of them. Far too often, he would be outside on the steps sitting when Nana BG and Hadea pulled up. Nana BG would notice that Hadea would call from her cell phone that her dad got for her, and she would call no names but would say that she was on her way home or she was home. Nana BG would see how he looked over at Hadea when they would take their evening walks. It should have not been a problem that Hadea liked a boy. However, this was a man. Shakira and Nana BG found out later that he was twenty years old.

By this time, Hadea was coming in the front door. She dryly greeted her mom, Justin and Nana BG. She walked straight to her room that she used while at Nana BG's and closed the door. Nana BG exclaimed that this is what she has to go through, and she should not have to. Hadea ended up coming out her room after twenty minutes or so and was pleasantly sociable. It was getting late and Shakira had to work the next day, she just wanted to stretch out and go to sleep. A good home cooked meal always put Shakira to sleep, especially if she stuffed herself. Before leaving Justin and Shakira spent some alone time with Hadea, sitting outside. Shakira stressed the issue of Hadea respecting Nana BG. She also told her to be patient, Justin and she were working on getting a place, but in the meanwhile, she needed Hadea not to go to battle with Nana BG. It was more like a warning; Nana BG was at her wits end with Hadea's mouth and her attitudes, there is no telling how or when Nana BG may become extremely angry and blow up on Hadea. Hadea acted as if she was in understanding and kissed Justin and her mom goodnight.

Since Justin and Shakira had a car now they parked next door to the storage facility at the restaurant/nightclub. There were cars outside that place sometimes all night long. Justin pushed the code in on the gate to open it. Shakira was right behind him. Before they got to their tin storage home, they saw Hassan coming back from doing his nightly rounds of patrolling the grounds. Mainly to make sure, all looks good and that no one is outside after hours.

Hassan walked over toward Justin with his hand extended to shake Justin's hand. Hassan let Justin know that he was going back to stay with his parents in hopes that he can get help with his drug habit. He said that his parents have hired a new manager. He claimed that she is a long time friend of his and that she already knew about the set up he had going on at the storage facility. Therefore, if they were to see her do not be alarmed, her name is Cheryl. Justin thanked Hassan and wished him the best, just in case he did not see him anymore after that day. Then Justin's mind went into thought, processing what

Hassan just said. He already knew there needed to be a plan in order.

The next day while at work Shakira heard her name paged over the intercom, alerting her that she has a phone call. She picked up the phone at the station where she was working. It was a detective of the gang unit at Hadea's school. Introducing his self as detective Coleman. He asked Shakira if she was aware of Hadea's whereabouts that day. As far as Shakira knew, Hadea should have been in school. Detective Coleman told Shakira that another officer picked Hadea up downtown a couple of hours ago. Hadea skipped school to hang out with a sex offender; fortunately, she was spotted by a friend of the family contacted the police. The male caught with Hadea was a registered sex offender who just violated his parole because of this incident. Making an illegal turn, an officer pulled the sex offender over, and disappointingly, the officer let go a known sex offender on a warning, "That high school kids' need to be in school, not riding around with an adult that is not a guardian". Tami went immediately to the schools police substation and identified herself as a family member and she was the one that called in. Tami asked if Hadea's parents were called, she was assured that they were and was told that they were on there way. Shakira was upset when she found out that the police stopped the offender and then let him go. Hadea was the center of it all. She had the answers to our "whys" but Hadea was not talking. In all, Shakira ended up getting off work early. Justin was already on his way since Detective Coleman called him first, and then he requested to get Shakira's work number so he could inform her.

They arrived at the schools police substation. As soon as Justin and Shakira opened and entered the small area in which it held three dark wood desks, each occupied. They walked in a little further and saw Hadea sitting off to the side in a chair. The officer, which sat in the desk positioned in the middle of the room, was Detective

Coleman as he introduced his self and motioned at the chairs for them to sit. They sat down and listened to Detective Coleman asking if they knew this male that Hadea was with, with only a name of Ronnie McCoy, and that did not ring a bell to neither Justin nor Shakira. Detective Coleman turned around to the printer sitting on a matching dark wood sofa table that sat against the wall. He swiveled back around to face Justin and Shakira and placed a photo mug shot in front of them. Shakira looked over at Hadea and shook her head. Indeed this same male lived near Nana BG. The same one Hadea had been lying about sneaking and seeing. Shakira was tired of all the hoops she had to jump through for Hadea, and she was still ungrateful of the love, attention, and guidance that Justin and Shakira gave to her. Shakira told the detective that she knows of this person living in the same apartments as her mom and how she, Justin and Nana BG all suspected for quite some time that he had been involved with Hadea. Hadea was fourteen when she started displaying her negative attitude and behavior toward Justin and Shakira. As Shakira thought back, she remembered Hadea mentioning the name Ronnie on several occasions, and when she asked Hadea the name of the male she kept eyeing as he passed she would say "Boogie". Shakira even told the officer how Nana BG approached Ronnie on two occasions and told him that he better not be trying anything with her granddaughter because she was a minor, and she sees how he seems to be outside each time they arrive home and how he watches her as she comes in his view. Ronnie was luckier than he knew. If Nana BG knew he was a pedophile she would have beat him down immediately, no questions asked.

By the time the Detective Coleman gathered all information, he received a call from his officers in the field. They found Ronnie McCoy at the address he been banned from base on the woman that lived there each had kids and Ronnie was not to be in the house with minors unless approved by his parole officer. Ronnie now headed downtown on a violation of his parole.

The next problem was with Hadea. The desk to the left of Detective Coleman belonged to the Gang Intervention and behavioral Students program, Dianna Shutice. She roused from her desk, came over, and introduced herself to Justin and Shakira. She added that Hadea was feeling at fault that Ronnie was in trouble. She tried to explain otherwise to Hadea, but she would not hear of it. Dianna had also told Justin and Shakira that Hadea said she did not care about school and she was going to drop out to become a strip dancer. Hearing this, Shakira felt her face melt away; she was embarrassed that Hadea would tell these people some crazy mess like that. Dianna had suggested academic probation for Hadea for six months, and she would have to check in every morning, lunch, and the end of the day to the police substation. She also suggested that Shakira check into teen council groups for Hadea; she said that some teens might need other teens going through the same issues in order to open up and cope with different problems. How blind Dianna was, Shakira thought. Maybe it was because Shakira knew how Hadea could manipulate the minds of adults. She knew what to say and how to put it to work in her favor. Teen counseling sounds good, but that was the lowest thing on the list needed for Hadea. She was hurt in so many ways inside; all signs pointed in the direction of self-destruction.

POINT OF NO RETURN

Hoping that this would be a wake up to Hadea, the ride to Nana BG's was a sullen one. Justin pulled into the lot and parked. Justin and Shakira opened their doors to exit the car. Hadea was still in the backseat starring out the window with a blank gaze in her eye. She acted as if she had not known that the car was no longer moving. Shakira told Hadea to get out the car several times, and each time Hadea refused. Justin knew Shakira wanted him to jump in and coach Hadea out the car but his lips was sealed. Justin knew from previous times not to get involved with battles involving Hadea. One last time, Shakira told Hadea to get out the car and before Hadea could smugly detest again, she was flying out the car before she knew it. Shakira reached in and pulled Hadea right out the car by the front of her shirt. That was enough for Hadea to start screaming from the top of her lungs, the things that she felt she could do to Shakira. Shakira ignored Hadea from that point on, she and Justin walked to the front door of Nana BGs with Hadea trailing beyond taunting Shakira as if they were feuding schoolmates. Nana BG had heard all the commotion and was already at the front door asking, "What's going on?" After Shakira told Nana BG the whole story, she was furious. Nana BG knew something was not right about the circumstance when she would see Hadea trying to capture the attention of this man. Nana BG would be outside, and would see on numerous occasions Hadea walking home and the older man pulling into his parking stall at least five minute behind Hadea. What shuck Justin and Shakira, was the fact that all Nana BG had done for Hadea she had the nerve to be walking around sneaking and lying like a snake.

While Hadea was in her room, the adults were still discussing the nerve of this child. What broke the mole was when Shakira told her mom where Hadea was going with Ronnie, aka the pedophile. According to Hadea, he was taking her to the clinic downtown to get some birth control pills. She claimed to have not been intimate with him and did not plan to be; he was more of a big brother who wanted her to be safe. With nothing said Nana BG flew off the couch so fast, she forgot about her aching senior bones. She was on a mission, a mission to tear into a nymphomania teenager smelling herself, as the old folk would say. Nana BG ordered Hadea to get out of the room. It took her two times to order Hadea out before Hadea appeared in the hallway. Nothing that came out of Nana BG's mouth was sugar coated. Her precious first grandchild was not ripe, she was rotten goods was one of Nana BG's colorful phrase's that brought on a power of rage to Hadea, she exploded like a Roman candle. Hadea was yelling, cursing and screaming like a truck driver locked out of his eighteen-wheeler. She started with Justin, went to Shakira and then Nana BG. Verbally lashing each of them in such a disrespectful manner. Shakira also had that unhealthy rage bottled in her as well, and the two together means a high voltage level. Shakira got up and told Hadea to shut her mouth; Hadea dared Shakira to make her do so. Overlooking Hadea's comment, Shakira went a different route on trying to defuse Hadea's rage. Until Hadea let one word too many slip from her naive lips and Shakira seem to have blacked out for a split second, before she knew it she had her five foot one, one hundred and nine pound petite frame pinned against Hadea, which jammed Hade up against the dining room table. From that, point on it was like watching an episode of Jerry Springer in 3D. Hadea stood at five feet six and weighed around one hundred and twenty five pounds so once Shakira no longer had control of Hadea her long arms, as they came swinging repeatedly as if she was swatting flies. Shakira did not want to hurt her only child but she would not calm down and quit jumping up in Shakira's face. Hadea came running up once more after

Shakira pushed her away. Shakira then swept Hadea right off her feet. Hitting the floor with a thud Hadea immediately started screaming that she was going to kill Shakira and then Justin. Nana BG had long eased into her room to slip into her sweats and take her wig off. She came out of the room and stepped behind Hadea; she was still on the floor, going through a tantrum of bottled of emotions. With Nana BG standing over Hadea as so, Hadea did not dare to move and that did not stop her from speaking her grief. Hadea was in the blame mode. She blamed Shakira for marrying Justin. As the tears ran from Hadea's eyes in a rhythmic pattern with her words, she spoke. She blamed Justin for taking her mom away and she blamed Nana BG for jumping to conclusions.

Although, Nana BG's conclusions about Hadea were all on point, Hadea refused to see the logic in it.

After about an hour of yelling, screaming and tussling exhaustion had settled in the air. Nana BG would have a good meal on by now, but with all the drama in her house cooking disappeared in her mental notes of things to do. Justin offered to go to KFC and get everyone something to eat. Nana BG got her purse, handed Justin a fifty-dollar bill, and told him to get whatever and keep the change. Justin turned down his mother in laws monetary offer and said he will take care of it. Justin kissed Shakira and left out the door.

While the attention had turned to food and not Hadea's foolish morals, she had gotten up off the floor and eased back into her room.

Shakira and Nana BG sat in the living room making sense of all the unanswered questions involving Hadea missing school, even after dropped off in the morning by Nana BG. Shakira figured out why Hadea let her grade point average drop down to a grade of a C. The direct root of Hadea's dysfunction, begin to unfold. Hadea was sixteen and still a little immature for her age. It was easy for Ronnie the predator to sweep little naïve Hadea of her feet. Hadea had it etched in her mind already that Ronnie did nothing wrong, in fact she felt guilty for his violation of parole being around a minor unsupervised and getting arrested.

Nana BG was not a violent person, but she had shown a malicious side from time to time. Her minds wheels where working overtime. Nobody messes with her family and not be dealt with. While in mid sentence of talking about Ronnie and how he needs to get what he deserves for being a pedophile and lying about his attentions with Hadea, Hadea leaped out from nowhere like a superhero and demanded that Nana BG and her mom shut up talking about business they know nothing about. Nana BG had been itching for months to get a piece of Hadea for all her lies, and sarcastic remarks; and this was the perfect opportunity. Shakira was on Hadea again. She was holding back on Hadea; she did not want to go brutal on her. Shakira was more so pushing Hadea away. Hadea and her wild fly movements caught Shakira off guard and she found herself in a headlock. Hadea did not care that this was her mom, all she saw was red hue over her target and she went for it each time she had a chance. Nana BG was right in on trying to control Hadea. The way she had Shakira in a headlock made it impossible for Nana BG to get Hadea without Shakira being in the way. Shakira broke a loose and without thought, popped Hadea right in the lip after Hadea had one last successful swing at her moms face, knocking her glasses off. That was it, Nana BG jumped in, do or die. She grabbed Hadea by her shirt collar and threw her down to the floor; Hadea was like a rubber ball bouncing back up in Nana BGs face so quick that Nana BG had a look of amazement on her face for a moment. Hadea grabbed Nana BGs hair and Nana BG grabbed on to Hadea's hair. The tug o' war battle ended when away came two of Nana BG's plaits of her hair in Hadea's hands. Hadea had French braids in and Nana BG had completely ripped out one from the side and completely pulled the top layer of one row up leaving plugs of hair still entwined into dangling braids that showed clean bald spots in various places of Hadea's head. Hadea rushed to the kitchen and grabbed a knife, she exclaimed that she would stab and cut herself and say that her mom and Nana BG attacked her. Nana BG could not believe her grandchild was disrespecting her. She ran as fast as her stubby 8WW bare feet would carry her. Bent over like a linebacker Nana BG ran full force toward Hadea. Hadea must have saw something in Nana BG that Shakira missed; because no longer did Hadea feel protected holding the knife, she dropped it like a hot potato and bolted for the front door. It looked as if she were going to run right through it, but somehow Hadea's coordination with her hands and agility in her steps led her to breakaway and run for her life. The door slammed right in Nana BG's face as Hadea ran screaming bloody murder through the housing community. Shakira stood motionless; she could not believe that Nana BG went toe to toe with Hadea in this manner. Shakira was mad at her mom; she dealt with this matter all wrong.

Justin had just missed scene one act eight. He opened the front door to a distraught look on his wife's face and tears in her eyes. He looked over to Nana BG who was sitting in her overstuffed lounge chair fussing. Shakira jumped up to help Justin put the bags in the kitchen. All he had to do was ask where Hadea was, and from there he would get the whole story. As to how she got to where she was now. Shakira was itching to tell Justin. Unfortunately, it was not surprising to him. Justin had told Shakira that Hadea would soon be trying to walk over her if she did not take control. That was when Hadea was ten, now she is fifteen. Shakira thought that Justin was being too hard on Hadea, which always led to a disagreement between the two of them.

Nana BG got up from her chair and tied her head rag on her head. She went to the kitchen and washed her hands before bringing down some paper plates from the cabinet. Nana BG was steaming mad; she told Shakira that Hadea could not stay with her anymore. Had she forgotten that Justin and Shakira were homeless? Nana BG was delirious with rage, she was not thinking clearly. Shakira just let her mom vent. After all, she was hurt that Hadea turned on her. She was doing so much for Hadea, unknowing that Hadea had plans only for manipulation and evil gain.

As Justin, Shakira and Nana BG sat, ate, and talked more about the windstorm of drama that Hadea stirred up. The three of them also had the opportunity to talk about the other issues. Shakira found out that Hadea was telling all kinds of lies to Nana BG against her mom and Justin, mostly Justin. Dreadfully, when she was with Justin and Shakira, she was telling lies against Nana BG. Normally parents are blind to their child's unworthy actions but in this case, Nana BG was the one that thought Hadea could do no wrong. She thought Hadea would never betray or disrespect her. Nana BG professed not to be bothered with Hadea, anymore. No longer will she worry about her having additional money to what she already gets. She will not worry about her getting to school on time anymore. In fact, Nana BG brought it up about Hadea continuing to live with her. Shakira reminded her mom that she was homeless. Nana BG cut in and said, "Homeless is having nowhere to go, can't she go stay in the storage with you and Justin?" It was evident that Nana BG had enough of Hadea this time. Her emotions had distorted her thoughts. She was not talking logical.

At that moment, the door opened and Hadea slid in cutting her eyes around the room, watching for any sudden movement. Shakira told Hadea she could get her something to eat. Hadea walked past her and said not a word. That was the cue for Nana BG to jump up and start talking about Hadea and her blemished character. Nana BG called Hadea a liar and that she would never trust her again. Nana BG spoke her peace and it made her feel good. After that, she sat back down to enjoy her meal. Like Flash Gordon Hadea flew out her room, ran up to Nana BG, and gave her three quick blows to the head before Nana BG jumped up and grabbed Hadea by her neck. Shakira and Justin jumped up, both almost knocking over the table where they had been eating. Shakira jumped between her mom and Hadea, Justin grabbed Hadea. Hadea knew Justin was not going to let her go, so she really made the show worth watching. Again, she was swinging her arms in the air and yelling. Nana BG told Shakira to move out her way. Shakira was not budging. Nana BG turned around and reached for her phone to call the police. Everything was happening so fast. Now the police were on the way. Shakira or Nana BG did not expect them to come so quick, but they did. There was a knock at the door and Shakira moved to open it. Occupying the opening of the door was three officers. Shakira notice one male and two female officers. There dark uniforms seemed to have made Nana BG's vibrant colored home turn dark as they stepped inside.

In Hadea's mind, she thought she needed to tell the officers her side of the story first. She blurted out to the officers as the water works started. Hadea told one of the female officers that her mom punched her in the face. She proceeded to show the officer her lip. She even told how Nana BG ripped her hair out. Swept under the rug was the fact that officers picked Hadea up earlier after spotted riding with a pedophile. No mention of her brandishing a knife and disrespecting the one's in her life that would do anything for her.

Although this was a serious matter, it was comical and adolescent when Nana BG sat up at the edge of her chair and said, "She beat me in the head and my head is sore!" Shakira had to hold back the sudden surge of laughter by biting her lip. Neither officer responded to Nana BG's accounts. It seemed, as no one knew what to say from there. However, thank God, Justin was there. He started to explain the day's events that may be the cause of this family vs. family war. Hadea could not contain her inside voice. She was straining her voice so much that the vain in her neck was protruding against her skin as to be ready to break out. She was like a record with a stuck needle. She whined that no one listens to her, her mom deserted her, and Justin is mean to her.

One of the female officers asked if she could use one of the other rooms to talk to Hadea. Shakira pointed toward the hall and said first door on the right. The female officer took Shakira to the front porch to hear her side of this evening's drama. Justin and Nana BG sat with the male officer to have their side of the report taken.

The female officer with Shakira had asked her multiple questions. For a moment, Shakira thought that was leading to her arrest, since she hit Hadea in the mouth and admitted to doing so. The officer must have been in Shakira's thoughts. She mentioned that that was not an issue. She was in agreement with Shakira keeping an unruly teen off her and out her face. This put Shakira at ease. Now the conversation was a little less guarded and the officer asked about what happened earlier and who were the officers working that case. Shakira answered the officer's questions as they were shooting from her mouth. At this point, the officer gave Shakira two options. One was juvenile hall or Hadea attends community services program for six months.

There was no doubt in Shakira's mind about being okay with sending Hadea to juvenile hall. That would be like sending a blind person into a den of hungry lions. Then the thought came across about their living arrangements. The female officer that was talking to Hadea peeked around the corner of the front door and whispered something to the officer Shakira was talking with, and then she was gone. The officer turned to Shakira and said, "Well, looks like we are taking her, she told my partner that she wants to kill herself and we cannot leave her if she is a threat to herself." Tears from nowhere immediately weld up in Shakira's eyes. Taking her where? Then, a response Shakira was not ready for almost dropped her to her knees. The officer told her they were taking Hadea in under a 5150 where she will be under a 24hr watch at the county mental hospital and from there, to a psychology center for young adults and teens.

Shakira followed the officer back inside, already Hadea was in handcuffs and the officer was explaining what they were going to do with Hadea to Justin and Nana BG. One of the officers pulled out a card and handed it to Justin. Moving toward the front door in hand cuffs and led by the officers' Hadea was quiet as a church mouse. Perhaps telling herself how she messed up and her manipulation game backfired on her. Hadea was positive that everyone else was at fault. Nana BG had lines of worry and heartache etched on her face. She doubted her actions and wondering if she did the right thing by calling the police.

Then they were gone. The house returned to its vibrant colors, yet, already it seemed to have already taken on the missing essence of Hadea. Shakira slid herself down on the couch next to Justin. Silence had engulfed the room. Nana BG was the first to speak, "Shakira, I know you did not want to see Hadea go, but maybe this will be a lesson to her to wake up". She continued to tell Justin and Shakira that under these circumstances they are going to need to be stable until they found out what is next for Hadea; she offered both Shakira and Justin to stay at her house. Under the condition, that they help clean and buy food. The agreement was that they had to be finding their own place, because whenever they release Hadea, Nana BG did not want her living with her anymore. Truth of the matter, she was now scared of Hadea and her irregular mood swings and blow-ups. Rationally, she could no longer trust Hadea on any level.

Looking at each other, Justin thanked his mother in law and said they will take it. Shakira was happy; this meant showers, food, and warmth all at her convenience. Words that are more shocking tickled Shakira and Justin's ears. Nana BG was apologizing to Justin for initiating evil behind him, using his name in vain around the family the way she did. She explained that she was going by what Hadea was saying and that she thought Shakira really tripped out and was letting Justin mistreat Hadea. Justin felt good. This was what he wanted to hear all along, he never meant any harm to anyone. He accepted his in laws as well as his owns family; but no one accepted him. Despite what Hadea stirred up, maybe this was a wake up call for a new start for them.

There is much more struggle, drama and dysfunction that Justin and Shakira must endure. The family is not through with them yet; and the devil still wants to play. Come back to laugh, cry, or even catch a bit of anger while reading a tale of dysfunctional love among family.

Family Gumbo, Volume 2
Coming soon!

Thank you Babe, for the guidance and teachings of spirituality. All the support and patience you provided kept me driven and strong. In addition, I thank you for staying strong as well and unbroken through it all, and for that, I Love you...

Family Gumbo

"Go to friends for advice;

To women for pity;

To strangers for charity;

To relatives for nothing".

- Spanish Proverb

www.ingramcontent.com/pod-product-compliance
Lightning Source LLC
Chambersburg PA
CBHW030642130626
46552CB00002B/972